My Lady Gambler

STORIES OF EROTIC ROMANCE, CORSETS,
AND AN ENGLAND THAT NEVER WAS

Victoria Pond

Cover by Anne Cain
Editing by Jennifer Levine
Copyediting by Rachel Solomon

ISBN-13: 978-0-9886468-2-7

Dueling a woman. Grandfather would be so disappointed.

"Ten!"

Stanley pivoted on a heel and presented a side-on target to his opponent, offering the smallest possible surface to the enemy. Perhaps a little dramatically, he raised his weapon one-handed in a straight line from shoulder to tip, feeling elegant in his frock coat and long muscles.

Clearly out of her depth, St. Cross mirrored the position.

"Fire!"

Stanley rotated the pistol from half-cock to full-cock and pulled, not letting the kick rock him. He felt St. Cross's bullet thump into the ground in front of him and looked down. How close that shot had come! He shifted back, away from the depression in the earth. Too close.

"Don't do this to me, old man."

Stanley looked towards the voice and froze. Althorp knelt, doubled over as though he'd been struck in the stomach. But he held the striking iron to him, for the metaphor was St. Cross—knocked down in her prime.

No, no, no. I missed! Stanley was sure of it.

ACKNOWLEDGEMENTS

Many thanks go to the writing critique group, Ladies of the Write, for all their feedback and for demanding the scene where Cara gets her masculine appendage. Also, I bow and scrape before my amazing editor, Jennifer Levine, without whom this book would make a lot less sense. And, of course, special thanks to Jeremy, my "main investor" and spouse.

CONTENTS

My Lady Gambler:

A Novella of the Late 18th Century

CHAPTER ONE – CARA ST. CROSS

Cara St. Cross could honestly say poker had saved her life. Without it, she'd have ended up working in some filthy den of iniquity, like any other country girl come to London. She was lucky to have the choice: work upstairs in the bordellos or play at the tables for her money.

But there was more to it than freedom from the flesh houses. She loved the rush of winning a large pot and the anxiety over losing her month's food money. Over the years, she'd worked her way up from little games in the lower city to earning a place at the Caller Club, home of the highest-stakes poker game in all England.

In the month since she'd acquired membership, gossip among the *ton* had yet to die down, although there was little to tell. *Have you heard about the woman who joined a gentlemen's club?* As a lucky happenstance, she rarely had to show a letter of introduction or proof of finances these days. Her fame opened doors as well as any title or ten-pound note.

She was a woman who loved poker, so she needed to join a gentlemen's club, *this* gentlemen's club. Nothing sordid to discuss, just a bit of costuming. And once she'd got in, the members politely chose not to notice the masquerade.

Yes, the Club was a glorious place, except when it came to food. Whatever possessed men to exist on a diet of meat and salt?

Cara slipped through the unassuming door that separated the elaborate, empty dining hall from the kitchens. She had yet to attempt it, but she felt sure that she could find a more edible species of victuals away from the common tables.

In stark contrast to the darkly appointed public area with its oak furnishings and Persian carpets, the kitchens had an air of efficient modernity. The floors mopped up easily in plain, white tile. All surfaces—from countertops to stove hoods—shone in silvery chrome. Electric lights lined the walls, and any number of gears turned raw ingredients into finished products. No pocketbook's strings had pulled tight when maximizing functionality here, just as no expenses would ever be spared when creating the opulence outside its doors.

Kitchen maids in voluminous skirts and near-medieval corsets loosed giggles from their bonneted heads—bonneted "to keep hair out of the food, miss"—when they caught sight of Cara. Resplendent in her oddness, Cara acknowledged their titters with an awkward wave of her fingers, then straightened her white button-down and perfectly gentlemanly black jacket.

Like many other gentlemen of the Club, she chose tails this evening—as every evening for the last month—glad for that little bit of propriety, that little bit of covering to keep the curves of her bottom hidden. A back-laced corset underneath her shirt and tie paid respect to her femininity, for all that her other trappings—from short blond hair to polished black boots—gave the opposite cultural signals. A costume that was part and parcel of getting into the Caller Club, so named for the building's owner rather than a fondness for calling on friends or ladies.

As far as the institution was concerned, Mr. St. Cross was a society gentleman. He had a house in the city; wore his clothes fashionably, if over ladies' foundation garments; and joined in activities from gaming to fencing. No secret was his true gender, but a polite fiction maintained for the sake of the rules.

In the kitchens now, Cara eschewed the young women who tried to catch her eye, seeking out an older face. Yes, someone older and less prone to flights of fancy. Someone less interested in the rumors surrounding the new, female member of the gentlemen's club. *Ah, there!*

She approached a woman with a lined face and a body more round than plump—the mark of a successful culinary practitioner. "Pardon, ma'am. Could I get a bite to eat? And to eat here in the kitchens? Nothing fancy, and nothing coated in gentleman's relish."

The woman pushed her gently towards a small table heavily pitted and coated in crumbs. "Sit yourself down, dearie. I know what you need."

From the way everyone else scrambled to fulfill the woman's desires, Cara knew she'd chosen someone high up in the hierarchy, maybe even the *sous chef.*

"Not another steak!" the woman called out to a young maid working the sizzle station.

Cara breathed a sigh of relief. Steak might've been just as bad as another slice of bread smeared liberally with that infernal anchovy paste. How much of that stuff could the regular members eat in a day?

A girl put a salad on the table, curtsied, and scampered away. Off to gossip with friends, no doubt, about the strange woman-man who ate vegetables and didn't demand extra salt. Next, a timid thing inched up. Her steady hand served a plate of boiled chicken and broccoli.

Cara took a bite of heaven. Her townhouse in London didn't have a full larder. It didn't have the space, being barely the size of a box, though in a newly fashionable neighborhood. She made sure to have a few things on hand, more for her servant-wards than for herself, but these upscale clubs had glorious food. She'd never known its like in the country nor in the lower-class gaming establishments.

Tonight, her chicken was moistened in its own juices, bursting with light spices and natural flavors. The boiled broccoli melted across her tongue with a green sort of flair, and the salad crisped along her palate in perfect complement to the smooth, creamy dressing. She caught the kitchen mistress's eye and tipped her head in thanks. She had the distinct sense that the old woman was laughing at her decadent enjoyment, but she couldn't muster the will to care about anything other than the spread before her.

At least, not until her gastronomic contentment was interrupted by a particularly bold maid. In the same graying skirt-and-bodice uniform as all the others, this maid still stood out. Her shiny chestnut hair wasn't caught up in a bonnet, and her broad eyes winked mischievously at anyone who had the fortune to fall under her gaze. A friend to girls and a friend to men, this maid clearly knew how to get her way with most people.

The maid slanted onto the bench beside her and wrapped an arm around Cara's shoulders. Her breasts heaved along Cara's arm, and her sweet, soapy scent wafted into Cara's nostrils, obscuring the taste of chicken slightly. The maid apparently had a technique for dealing with members who came down to the kitchens possibly looking for a bit of fun, but Cara was no usual member, and she merely wanted to eat before joining the tables.

"Is it true?" the maid asked in a husky voice. "Does your metal appendage work just as well as the real thing?"

If Cara knew one thing, it was *always be polite to the kitchen staff.* So she patted the maid's hand and said, "It gets me in upstairs and allows for the expelling of bodily fluids," before she took another bite of her meal. Would that be enough to assuage curiosity?

All the women shamelessly listening in tittered at this bit of gossip, and Cara's burr pressed closer to her side. "So, you've tested it out then. Care to give it another go?"

She was truly being propositioned! Best to nip that in the bud. "Ah, it does not have *that* particular function. I referred earlier to, ah, conjunctive fluids, those familiar to both men and women."

Seemingly undeterred by this description, the maid reached down into Cara's trousers and tapped at her metal masculinity with a fingernail. "Seems stiff enough to me."

Cara looked down to see her trousers gaping and a hand running over the plates and bolts of her technical penis.

"I bet you know all the ways to please a woman." The maid smoldered from under sooty eyelashes, probably thinking she'd reap her reward now.

Though the touch sent no sensations through her body, Cara knew she could use this to her advantage. The maid had crossed a line, one she should never have tested so openly.

Cara stood abruptly, playing the part of the offended gentleman with every contriving bone in her body. "I *beg* your pardon!" she cried in a tone that did nothing of the sort. With a wounded dignity, she tucked her extra appendage back into her dress trousers and waxed furious at the whole room. "To think, that you would make free with my body and belongings! A member of the Club! I shall speak with my sponsor about this, posthaste!"

She wouldn't, of course, speak with her sponsor, an aging earl who'd lost an unnamed favor to her in a Belfast poker game last year. As far as the men were concerned, randy kitchen girls who reached for your slap-and-tickle while providing your meal should be the standard. But the would-be seductress didn't need to know that. She only needed to assimilate Cara's displeasure and walk away from trouble.

Just like Cara herself should do. Already standing, she tugged her jacket sleeves down to their tailored extent, resting at her slender wrists and above the white cuffs. She made a cursory bow to the kitchen mistress and strode haughtily from the room, still trying to channel the right sort of affronted attitude.

Behind her, she heard scolding and screeching, but she blocked it out. She'd been well fed, was well dressed, and would be well heeled by the end of the evening.

Back through the empty dining room she went. Then through the library, careful not to trip into any freestanding globes or pedestals with ostentatious busts of long-dead generals; somehow these baubles seemed more prolific than books, but that could have been due to their unfortunate tendency to get in her way.

Another door, and she'd found her place. Woodcuts decorated the walls with subtle artistry, difficult to appreciate since the fireplace had gone dark. Only the gaslamps on the gaming table's corners remained lit. She crossed the room to a small bar. As she poured herself a glass of dark port—older than her dead parents, for certain—she calculated the odds at the table. Two seats were open, but did she wish to sit in?

The earl, her patron, shuffled his cards between his hands, an obvious sign of a fine hand, but one only she and the grinning Viscount Althorp recognized. Beside the earl and the viscount sat Count Demidov, visiting from the Russian Empire, and Mr. Williams, who'd bought his way into the Club with his father's railroad investment money.

Althorp folded and placed his cards on the table, acknowledging her attention with a wry smile. "Not my night, is it, St. Cross?" he asked her. "I've lost that round to my lord, and now you appear to further relieve me of my well-won gains."

With an invitation like that, she had to join the table, even if the remaining two players were dangerous amateurs. Most members of the Club fell into such a class, so she didn't let it stop her. She'd gone to the effort of winning the earl's favor, then had learned the way to make herself acceptable under the Club's charter. All for the sake of joining the highest-stakes poker game in the British Isles.

So, even if the loosest, most passive poker players in the world sat in those other chairs, she still would play against them. She would test her skill, test her luck, and win her way to the only thing that mattered: the knowledge that she had played here and won. She grabbed a set of green-colored chips and swung into the seat beside her friendly rival.

The amateurs finished up their round, with the earl winning, and Althorp handed her a fresh deck, still in its factory casing. At the Caller Club, they took any possibility of cheating seriously. "New man deals," said the viscount.

Each player tossed in ten thousand pounds for the ante. Cara's heart beat faster. *Ten thousand pounds!* She could have bought her parents' home and livestock twenty times over with money to spare. How her situation had changed.

Five shuffles—as gaming houses properly required—and she dealt out five cards to each man. While they deliberated over which to part with, she looked at her own hand. *Ugh.* Pair of deuces, ten high. She'd keep the pair and toss the rest. She led the round of bets and checks. Then, one by one, the players traded their cast-offs for shiny new pasteboard.

From the hallway, she heard the sharp snap of hard soles marching across wood floors. The walker moved in a furious rhythm, easily outpacing the doorman whose flurry of remonstrating babble—which didn't seem *too* protesting—carried into the card room. The man belonged here, then; he was just in a foul mood. With any luck, he'd head straight to the library or the billiards room. Most all the poker regulars sat next to her already.

She'd just dealt the earl two new cards when the door burst open; yellow light from the hall backlit the newcomer like a painted halo around a portrait of Jesus. She knew the man, of course. Stanley, Marquis of Greenhope, was a long-standing member of the Club, though she'd never heard of him showing up like this.

Unlike the other members in attendance, Lord Greenhope didn't wear tails or frock coat. His white shirt had no collar and was grayed with sweat. His lower legs encased in riding boots that showed off shapely calves, horsewhip still in his hand, the man didn't appear to belong. After all, the sleeping rooms above were always stocked with clothing in each member's size in order to avoid exactly this sort of sartorial mismatch. Whyever had he let himself be seen in such a state, forcing his way in without stopping to change?

"You!" bellowed Lord Greenhope. "You thief of women!" His otherwise handsome face turned red as he roared. "You mockery of a man!" In an athletic bound, he smacked his whip down on the table in front of Cara, scattering cards and chips, putting a definite halt to the game.

She tensed in an attempt to keep still, not daring to move.

Viscount Althorp leaned back in his chair, seeming to sprawl even more comfortably. He tutted like a school mistress. "Now, now, Greenhope. Can't this wait till after the hand?"

So close, Cara could see the planes of Lord Greenhope's chest, peeking through the now-transparent shirt he wore. A droplet of sweat fell from his heaving shoulders and onto her fingers. She rubbed it into her skin, liking the sensation of simultaneous hot and cold, reveling in the knowledge that she'd stolen this silky piece of him. The marquis in high dudgeon had a magnetism, and she couldn't help but want to be closer, though she knew she ought to get very far away indeed. No one wanted to be the focus of such fury.

Lord Greenhope pointed directly at her, as sure an insult as any. "Pistols at noon tomorrow, Bunhill Fields. You will be there."

Bunhill Fields. A cemetery. He meant to bury her? Like Hell she'd be there! Then again, her position in this society trembled on a tenuous crest of honor. If she refused a duel, would she be unmanned and made unfit for membership in this rarefied institution? In that case, she'd fight for her right to remain. But, God in Heaven, she didn't want to die! "May I ask," she said, "what this is all about?"

Lord Greenhope snarled, his red, robust countenance gone a pasty white. "I arrived home this evening to be informed in no uncertain terms that *my wife* has been having relations with another man." His pointed gaze left no doubt as to the alleged identity of that other man.

Althorp and the earl didn't look at all convinced, going far enough to wrinkle their brows. She loved them intensely for this showing of disbelief against their social peer in her favor.

Ever the brave one, Althorp asked the question she couldn't force through her shock-locked jaws. "Whatever makes you think St. Cross is the culprit?"

Lord Greenhope leaned over the table, getting as close as he could to this new adversary. Starting in a whisper, he replied, "Because Lady Greenhope said her lo-ver—" His voice cracked on the word, as if he couldn't bear to say it. "Her lover fucked like a machine."

He wheeled on Cara and pointed at her again, this time with the horsewhip. "You are the only mechanical man I know," he said. "And I will have satisfaction." With that, he stormed from the room, collecting his hat from the doorman as he passed.

Cara sat in silence for a moment, then went to work collecting the strewn cards. She reshuffled five times. Then six. Then seven. Had she managed to find the whole deck? What if there were cards still on the floor?

The earl handed her a fresh deck and patted her shaking hand. "No help for it then."

Althorp nodded, the movement bouncing his hair's lustrous queue. "I'll stand your second." For all that they'd only made acquaintance five weeks before, she counted Althorp her most stalwart friend.

Noon at Bunhill Fields. Either she'd get in a lucky hit or Lord Greenhope would shoot her dead.

* * *

The earl's phaeton dropped her in front of her respectable townhouse in Shaftesbury Square, a recently gentrified section of Battersea. Her residence—purchased before the gentrification, when everything was opium dens and starving artists—stood two stories, both of them tiny but neatly kept. She only had so many possessions to clutter the place, after all. Some *nouveau riche* liked to surround themselves with newfound opulence, others never got used to owning too much. Cara stood firmly in the second category.

She alighted from the carriage on sure footing, leather boots hitting the cobbles with a *thud.* Then she leapt the few brick steps to her plain wooden door, its thickness and two inset panels showing more function than beauty, but enough to make her a reasonable acquaintance in polite society.

Just get inside. She rapped on the door hard enough to bruise knuckles. She'd have to get a cane soon.

Her butler-cook-ward, Nathan, opened the door, and

she rushed in, trusting the young man to wave off the driver. She streaked past him and up the stairs, heading for her private room. He wouldn't worry about her yet. She'd made mad dashes before... in a hurry to use the wash closet without her metal manhood.

But that wasn't the case tonight. Tonight, she needed to get out of this ridiculous outfit, to put some distance between herself and *Mr. St. Cross*, who had a duel tomorrow.

A duel! They were barely legal these days, and she'd never anticipated involvement in one. Yes, gentlemen postured and held them, a few a year, but always young bucks out to impress their mates. Not the kind of lads you'd find at the Caller Club, with its stodgy sitting rooms and old-moneyed members.

She reached for her tie, splendidly behind the fashion in unflamboyant white. *Perdition!* The knot refused to come undone. Flushed, heat rising, knowing she'd cool off if only she were free of it, she tried to get her fingers between the folds. She yanked and tugged, but to no avail, just the promise of bruises if she kept it up.

Her tiny bedroom had only a small bed and a large vanity, more necessity than decadence. She stood in front of the mirror, then opened the second mahogany drawer on the vanity's right. *Where was it?* She rummaged for a pair of scissors or a straight razor. Anything to cut through this damned Gordian Knot.

A knock came on her chamber door.

"Miss?"

That was Mindy, Cara's younger ward-valet. Cursed with a sweetly round face and blue, wide eyes, Mindy had a perfectly guileless look. It was a look tailor-made for a child who picked pockets or an adult who fleeced johns, and not suitable for any other professions in a city-woman of low means. After barely saving her own purse from separation two years ago, Cara had taken the adolescent girl home with her instead of leaving her to her fate. As a former prostitute-to-be herself, she hoped Mindy would turn this favor onto another young girl someday.

Warm fingers captured the knife shaking in Cara's grasp. When had Mindy got so close?

"Let me help you out of this, miss." Mindy didn't wait for approval. Efficiently, without slicing, she stripped Cara's tie and removed her diamond cufflinks, then her jacket and shirt.

Somehow, Cara found herself standing while her valet divested her of the trousers and socks that finished her manly raiment. Next, the laces of her corset, a beautiful gold-and-blue jacquard that only she and Mindy saw these days.

Finally, she wore nothing but long limbs and chrome cock. This metallic madness! Anyone could see it for the joke it was. A frippery. A silly convenience to get around the rules. Yet it had forced her into this insanity. This token of male anatomy made her a *machine*, and Greenhope would kill her for it.

Shivering in her bare skin, she barely restrained from striking it. All that would do was pull at things that shouldn't be pulled.

Why? She felt tears welling up, but didn't let them fall. Why did Lord Stanley have to pick *her*? She understood his need to reclaim his honor, but no one could possibly think she'd slept with Lady Greenhope.

The damned piece of scrap didn't work that way!

Her fingers jerked at the belt buckle that secured her penis's position, and she kept tugging after the hook slipped its ring, squeezing her waist roughly with the thick leather and pinching her skin against the clasp. That little pinch stung like a welt, like Greenhope's horsewhip, like all the worries she had over how on Earth to shoot a pistol.

Tears ran from her eyes, and her cheeks were immediately sore with scrunching. How was she going to do this? What did she know about duels? Did this make

Greenhope her lifelong enemy? Althorp her bosom friend? Would she be dismissed from the Caller Club?

She collapsed onto her bed like Punch or Judy after the audience has gone home, one prudent hand on her cock her only concession to cognizance. She shook and tried not to writhe, her coverlet soaked a darker blue where tears had fallen. When only heaving sobs remained, she became aware of Mindy's hands running through her short hair, the soothing whispers above her head.

With a last sniffle, Cara stood again, somehow feeling calmer, ready to face the world. Whatever would happen would happen. She'd already come so much farther than she'd ever thought, leaving the country farms and the cheap dens of iniquity behind her. Her achievements were her own, and no one could take them away. Being sent down from the Caller would be the worst of all possible worlds. She just had to stay alive, and how likely was Greenhope to shoot to kill? Not very.

Steadily this time, she loosened the first belt, the one that controlled the finest movements of her penis. The waist strap already unbuckled, she released the garter-like clasps on her inner thighs, then slipped the whole outer cage off, leaving the main structure still attached. Mindy picked the enclosure up off the floor and hung it over the back of a chair. She'd condition the leather and hang it more neatly later, but the second step for complete removal required two pairs of hands.

Cara grasped the shaft, careful not to get stuck in any of the rivets. Rivets. The whole *metal penis* idea had been a disaster from the start.

The first contraption had been more snakelike and disjointed. That hadn't worked so well. It had been her second trip to the Club, her first with the shiny cock under her voluminous skirts. If you hadn't known it was there, you wouldn't have been able to learn by looking. The doorman wasn't best pleased about the skirts and had told her to go up the stairs and change into proper attire. She'd been admitted, though, now that he could tell she was a man in truth. Well, a man in *fact*, leastwise.

Ridiculous strap-on or not, she'd got in! She'd been allowed past the door this time, not like the first time when she'd been turned away and the earl had been strongly cautioned that *eccentric* could easily shade into *lapsed membership*. If she hadn't got in on the second try, she had no doubts that the earl would consider his debt to her discharged and leave her to fend for herself, unable to wend her way into the highest-stakes poker game in all Britannia.

Upstairs in the members' dressing rooms, she'd seen the male attire and nearly swooned. Did the Club truly expect her to dress as a man? Bad enough they'd made her become a man in apparatus, though she could under-stand the need to keep a gentlemen's club by gentlemen and for gentlemen. But, still. Wasn't enough enough?

Clearly not, so she'd rummaged through the lot and steeled herself to show an improper amount of figure. Not that it would really matter. She'd worn similar things in the fields of her parents' farm, and she'd worn more scandalous attire when first learning to deal for card players more interested in the goings-on upstairs than down in the card room.

She'd chosen a frill-chested button-down and a very billowy frock coat. Mix them with an unmatched pair of trousers, leave on her own gloves and socks, and that should do well enough. She'd look a fright, she'd been sure, but what did she really know about men's fashion?

Unlacing her corset, she'd been grateful she'd worn a front-laced one on this occasion. How little she'd known! The corset had come off just fine, but then the struggle with her skirts started. Something kept getting caught and jerking her body in circles. Since all the skirts were at-tached to each other—an invention to make her dressing easier on young Mindy—catching one meant catching them all.

She'd tugged and pulled. She'd turned around in circles like a dog chasing its own tail. In the end, she'd ended up with a shredded set of underskirts. At least the top one had come out of the mess all right, and she'd later been able to patch up the petticoats.

Finally free of the skirts, she could see the damage. Bits of cotton had wedged between the articulated joints of her penis—really a broken, armored glove from a second-hand shop—and left it bent all out of shape. Lumpy here, twisting right there, then left again. An abomination. Moreover, she couldn't put her dress back on.

Deciding to brazen it out, she'd first put on the peacock shirt—but without a corset, her breasts had been hanging free. With each breast a bit larger than her fist, this meant they'd set to swaying and would be horribly sore by the end of the evening. But she could handle it.

She could've handled it.

But then she had to put on the trousers. Thankfully, they'd been designed for a man with a larger tackle than her glove. Less thankfully, she'd had to put them on with no undergarments, and they'd pushed the edges of her metal piece tight against the crotch. She could see slivers of silver beginning to protrude from her slacks, and she had felt metal pushing against her lower belly quite uncomfortably.

With a stroke of inspiration, she'd wrapped the tool in a strip from her massacred skirt and then put on another layer of trousers. And then another layer, just to be safe.

By the time she'd emerged from the dressing room, she'd been wearing six pairs of trousers, an engorged penis, a floppy shirt, and a frock coat so billowy that she could've worn twenty more pairs of slacks without anyone's noticing.

Utterly aghast, the earl had sent her home and told her in no uncertain terms that their association was done unless she managed to get herself in by some other means.

For the week following the debacle, she'd worked on both her metal penis and her ensemble. Luckily, the doorman had recognized her when she'd next reappeared with a better cock and a very suitable wardrobe for a young gentleman about town.

Perhaps her current metal manhood, commissioned from a sculpture artist who lived in the more industrialized section of Battersea, wasn't greatest work of art, but it *worked.* A gently up-curved cylinder, it had been cobbled together from any number of leftover pieces of steel and chrome and aluminium. But shape only made half the beauty of this piece. The other half: functionality.

No, it wasn't pleasant, and she hated putting it on or taking it off. But a slightly tapered tube could be inserted, meaning that a lady with a great deal of pelvic muscle could relieve herself through the permanently stiff cock. For obvious reasons, she tried to hold out, but every now and then, something... came up, so to speak.

"Come hold this, Mindy," she summoned her teenage assistant. "You hold, and I'll pull. One, two, three!"

And with a piercing squelch of discomfort, the tube was removed and the metal with it. Last, she unwound the silk from her lower body, a protective material to keep the sharp metal edges from tugging at her pubic hairs or scoring lines into her skin.

Totally naked, she gloried for a moment in her freedom from the device, from the pretense of acting like a man when everyone knew her to be a woman. Then she pulled on a silk robe. It was all worth it. Worth it when she got dealt in.

Mindy already had the oils and cleaning basin out, so she left the girl to it and went to find Nathan. He was sitting in the kitchen, a mug of hot tea in his hands, staring morosely into the swirls he created when he tipped it one way and then the other. Well, she could take his mind off his problems by discussing her own.

"So, Nate. What do you know about duels?"

The surprised look he gave her wasn't very comforting.

* * *

Dearest Althorp came by at eight the next morning, four hours before they were due at Bunhill Fields, and he'd brought an assortment of armory with him. Though she'd made a few visits to his London apartments at the Tower, she'd never been subjected to his ballistics collection. His bouncing enthusiasm for the pieces proved that she should have asked about the weaponry before.

"We've discussed your fencing before, old man," he said—she'd taken up swordplay as her martial art when she'd taken up her gentleman role—"but I wasn't sure if you had any particular pistol you'd like to use."

She hadn't known that he thought her this close a friend. He knew quite well that she didn't have a pistol, rifle, or cannon of any kind, yet here he was pretending that she was just like any other man for whom he might stand second.

"I didn't have one in mind," she said. "Would you care to make a recommendation?"

He crossed to her parlor table and opened the first of the three tooled, wooden boxes he'd set upon it. Inside, nestled in crimson velvet, lay a small wood-and-gold pistol, with scrollwork decorating the grip. She'd have called it a *ladies' derringer* except that it had six rotating chambers, clearly to be turned by some mechanism based on a bulb of gas at the top of the stock. Along the top, two loupes made for precision sighting. She'd never seen anything so beautifully deadly, and, at that size, she might even be able to handle it.

Then he opened the second box to reveal something significantly longer, perhaps qualifying more as a rifle rather than a handgun. Stretched and thin, its cork-screwed barrel undoubtedly meant something to the serious practitioner, but Cara had no idea what it was for. Perhaps this was rendered moot by the tripartite aiming system with dual holes through a scrollcap that lined up with a lens at the end. Or perhaps not.

She looked on with interest as Althorp displayed the third and last box. Unlike the other two, this box looked relatively plain, only painted in patterns rather than engraved and built up. Much simpler, this gun's stock and base were solid wood, unembellished. The barrel itself, the trigger, and the gascap were made of hard, corrosion-resistant chrome. For a sighting system, though, this one seemed the most complex, with what looked to be a tiny telescope attached to the side.

Althorp bowed to her. "My belongings, as my life, are at your disposal."

Oh dear. What was she supposed to say to that? Since the beginning, Althorp had treated her like any other gentleman of the Caller. Where others had seen a woman in pantomime costume, where some in town had treated her like a trollop, where most members of the Club had taken a few days to get used to her strange ways, Althorp had neither needed to adjust nor got the wrong idea. They'd visited each other's homes with no chaperones nor concerns for propriety.

Maybe she was misinterpreting. Maybe men became bosom friends when going into duels together. Please, God, let that be the bond they shared. For, while he was a handsome man and sharp with cards, she hadn't come to London in order to marry or tarry. She'd come to play poker. With a gentleman of the Club, well… it couldn't be a mere dalliance, or else she'd risk expulsion when it ended.

No, she was better off entering a relationship with anyone *except* Althorp—or the earl or the rest of that set.

Unsure how to respond, she gazed at the pistols, their comparative properties a confounded mystery to her.

Young Nathan saved her from having to continue the viscount's line of conversation—and she'd bet he derailed the topic on purpose; her wards were utterly devoted. "If it please you, miss," he said, playing up his waif-like appearance and speaking far more politely than he would have done if they had been alone, "Mister Claxton what owns the Claxton Hotel out in Bloomsbury says I can run his errands and learn about the hotelling trade, miss. If you could split my hours with Mindy, miss, I'd be right grateful."

Nate was laying it on thick for their guest, all right, not that Althorp hadn't already grown used to the somewhat lax manners of her household with its modest staff of street urchins. She barely tamped down on her laughter. She also hoped he was serious about Mr. Claxton wanting his help. Her servants would have all the opportunities she—and they—could scrape for them, and Nate would appreciate this one all the more for having got it on his own.

"Of course you may," she told him, playing the benevolent mistress just as well as he'd played the down-and-out street child. "We'll discuss your schedule as soon as I finish this business." Then she turned her attention back to the pistols on the table. She heard the echoes of fading footsteps and knew that Nate had disappeared into the kitchen.

Althorp was hovering next to the ladylike weapon, which, hopefully, had the least kick. She took that as a sign, much as she wanted to ask about them all.

"I'll take that one," she decided. "And God help us if I need to fire it."

CHAPTER TWO – LORD GREENHOPE

This is a farce, thought Stanley. He stood with his brother on a short pathway in front of a grey mausoleum, trying not to squint in the afternoon's cloudy glare. He could only hope to see his opponent through all this reflection; otherwise he might hit something, like a gravestone or a griever. Or Mr. St. Cross, whom he fully intended to miss.

He and his brother had both dressed for the occasion in Greenhope's colors: an ironic sapphire and silver with not a hint of green. They looked quite splendid, if he did say so himself, if far too bright for mourners in their saturated blue frock coats.

In a nod to the solemnity of the location, they held their top hats in their hands, showing off matching crops of dark brown hair. There the similarities ended, for Stanley was a tall, muscular man, sinewy and thick from riding and periodically working in his own shipyards. His younger brother had a more svelte figure, pencil thin with the look more of an accountant than a knight—technically—of the realm.

Whatever had possessed Stanley to pick this place? What an insult to the spirits of the dead to threaten an addition to their number, stirring up trouble in their place of rest. Really, though, the question ought to have been: Whatever had possessed him to challenge St. Cross?

For, though he couldn't identify his wife's lover, he could be reasonably sure that St. Cross was not the man in question. He'd looked too shocked. Honor was well and good, but where was the honor in frightening the poor man—worse to think of St. Cross as a woman in this context—and dragging him out to a fight to the death, for all he knew, in the middle of the afternoon?

It was all very inappropriate, and, in these calmer moments, Stanley rather thought he'd be better off spending time with his shipmasters and bookkeepers on matters of business. Poor St. Cross must be terrified! And few outcomes to this event could do him any good.

"Here they come," his brother said in an exquisitely bored drawl, pointing out two gentlemen coming up the walk.

Viscount Althorp led. Although older than the rest of the day's players by six or seven years, Althorp fairly bounded along the stone pavers. The Duke of Oxford's second son, Althorp had left the ancestral pile for a brief career as a high-ranking Navy officer, but had recently returned to play the dissolute rake in London for reasons so cloaked in secrecy that rumormongers were immediately shushed. Stanley recalled that the lord had won each of his youthful duels with a shot to his opponent's leg and fervently hoped Althorp hadn't been coaching St. Cross in such proclivities.

St. Cross herself—himself, damn it; so much easier to remember that when one couldn't see her... him— followed more slowly, obviously reluctant. She—*he!*— carried a box in his palm unsteadily, like a serving platter laden with overfilled wine goblets.

When the pair came to a shuffling stop a few feet away from him, he wished he could contrive to call the whole thing off. Althorp clapped St. Cross on the back, and the woman—*man, damn it!*—went sprawling forward. Stanley's brother caught the tooled wooden box St. Cross carried, and Stanley managed to right the young cardsharp with much patting of shoulders and *steady on*s.

They stood a few more minutes, St. Cross shuffling his feet, Althorp bouncing, and the Greenhopes keeping as perfectly still and straight as they'd been taught by their highly competent governesses. No hint of improper upbringing in that fine household, oh no.

"Well." Althorp's giddiness did not spill over to the day's other participants. "Let's get on with it, then."

With an apologetic grimace to St. Cross, which seemed to alarm her—*him!*—rather more than create a conspiratorial atmosphere, Stanley turned to his brother who, quite by chance, held both of the duel's weapons. He'd be playing moderator, then, as well as second.

First, that worthy opened St. Cross's box, revealing a snub pistol with an automatic rotation bulb. Capital. St. Cross checked the weapon, had Althorp load it with powder and a single bullet, and then brought it to rest against her—*his*, damn it—marvelously tailored trouser seam. Stanley rather thought he might ask after the man's tailor when this was all over, if he'd be willing to divulge the secret of his elegant lines.

Second, his brother opened the case he'd carried himself to display Stanley's firearm, a French piece covered in filigree and *fleurs de lis*, but a basic single-shot sidearm. His grandfather had carried it in the war to reopen the Nipponese sea lanes for the British in the early 1700s, and it had none of the fancy engineering seen in more modern weaponry.

Stanley checked and loaded his own pistol, then primed the flashpan, while the two seconds laid swords upon the top of a gravestone in case of necessary tie-breakers. *What a shame to bring such violence to a place of peace. Then again, maybe the dead have grown bored with the eternal niceness of the Fields.*

Back to back, they waited for the next direction. Stanley could feel St. Cross's tremoring shoulders, little points of heat that touched against him and then fluttered away again. A tantalizing tease that hinted at warm blood and solid muscles, but pulled that comfortable touch out of reach too soon.

The trembling also agitated the air, and Stanley scented the light soap and Brilliantine that proclaimed a fastidious masculinity. Though, of course, St. Cross wasn't masculine at heart and never pretended to be. Oh Lord. He'd challenged a woman to a duel. Grandfather would be so disappointed in him.

He inhaled deeply, half to calm his now-racing nerves and half to try and smell whatever lurked beneath her hair tonic and spicy Pears soap. Perhaps a hyacinth perfume or a hint of rose water. Or perhaps he deluded himself into thinking he could discern such things when the lady instead rested in a practical sort of femininity that included kohl-enhanced eyes and a well-shaped figure underneath her gentleman's finery.

"One!"

Stanley took a step forward automatically before his mind caught up and realized that his brother had called the first mark. The traditions of dueling commenced. *No way out now.*

"Two!"

Stanley took another step. This far away, he could neither feel nor smell St. Cross, but he heard her footfalls upon the gravelly ground.

"Three!"

And so on. They measured their paces like meticulously cut boards. Stanley put aside his apprehension and sunk himself into observing the forms perfectly. He had only to breathe and walk and turn and shoot into the distance.

"Ten!"

He pivoted on a heel and presented a side-on target to his opponent, offering the smallest possible surface to the enemy. Perhaps a little dramatically, he raised his weapon one-handed in a straight line from shoulder to tip, feeling elegant in his frock coat and long muscles.

Clearly out of her depth, St. Cross mirrored the position.

"Fire!"

Stanley rotated from half-cock to full-cock and pulled, not letting the kick rock him. He felt St. Cross's bullet thump into the ground in front of him and looked down. How close that shot had come! He shifted back, away from the depression in the earth. Too close.

"Don't do this to me, old man."

Stanley looked towards the voice and froze, pausing in returning his pistol to its place of rest. Althorp knelt, doubled over as though he'd been struck in the stomach. But he held the striking iron to him, for the metaphor was St. Cross—knocked down in his prime.

No, no, no. I missed! Stanley was sure of it. The bare idea of hitting a target he hadn't aimed towards with an antique pistol? Pure applesauce.

He tossed the firearm to his brother, who fumbled to catch it, and rushed to Althorp and St. Cross. The lady laid half on the ground and half in the viscount's lap, clearly unconscious. He inspected her for blood, taking in the shapely curve of her calf and the feminine row of tiny buttons at her waist. No blossom of vermillion nor droplet of heart's production anywhere upon her.

Althorp tapped her cheek, and this time she shook her head to escape the irritant. "Ahoy, there," the viscount said gently, his gaze trained on hers as though a coal-enforced pipe welded them together.

Stanley felt a bit the voyeur for watching such a tender moment, but he couldn't look away. Not until he knew of a certain that St. Cross had survived. The man didn't deserve pain and death at Stanley's own mal-judged pistolry.

Also, he wasn't sure the fallen of their number would want to be wrapped up in so intimate an embrace, though it wasn't his place to interfere if she did, of course. Then again, she'd chosen Althorp to stay her second, so perhaps his own interference stood unwelcome.

Her eyelids flickered a few times, then opened abruptly. Her face flushed a deep red, and Stanley fancied he could feel the heat of it from where he stood. Almost absentmindedly, she patted Althorp's hand on her cheek—both acknowledgement and dismissal at once.

Stanley offered his help in standing and felt a jolt when their palms met, a jolt even greater than the kick of his pistol only moments ago. In their bare moment of contact, he felt the dry surety of her palm and the delicacy of her relatively small frame.

"Thank you, sir," she said as she reclaimed her hand from him. He hadn't even noticed he'd held it overlong.

"Good to see you on your feet," said Althorp, but his words seemed out of place, as though only Stanley and St. Cross existed in this space and no one else belonged. Althorp's desire to worm himself into their world was not unwelcome, *per se*, but it was certainly irrelevant.

Stanley nodded his head in agreeable acknowledgement. "It gladdens me to know you remain unhurt." He tried not to notice the shocked flight of St. Cross's eyebrows, preferring to concentrate on less shame-inducing objects such as Althorp's comradely arm around St. Cross's shoulders. Stanley stifled a laugh at Althorp's transparency.

"Shall we off to drench our victory then?" Althorp invited them both. "I know of a new, Nipponese-themed club where we can drink our continued, collective health in peace." Ever since Tanuma Okitsugu had convinced Shogun Tokugawa Ieharu to end the Dutch monopoly on oriental trade by expanding Nippon's own shipping lanes into Europe, a small number of themed establishments had cropped up. Three in London alone.

Stanley couldn't leave his brother out of the oiling machine. "Care for a nip?" he asked the younger Greenhope. His reward was a withering look before his brother gathered up their things and made his way to the horse-drawn carriage in which they'd arrived. He couldn't say he'd expected his second, who only attended the main event out of familial duty, to join them. "Just the three of us, then."

* * *

Viscount Althorp did indeed know of a Nipponese-themed club, though Stanley didn't think you'd find anywhere like it on that oriental isle. They exited the street through a wooden gate that looked like a log version of Stonehenge, if the crosspieces curved up at the ends. To enter the establishment, they opened a red lacquered door, ornately carved in dragons and phoenixes which seemed more Chin than Rising Sun.

A person of indeterminate gender shuffled to greet them on legs encased in multiple constraints of columnar silk and balancing atop shoe-stilts that each had but two lines of contact with the ground. Its long, black hair—surely a wig—was piled artfully atop its head in ascending buns, and its face shone a pure white with black drawn eyes and red lips slashing through the starkness.

With bows and contralto instructions, the trio found themselves ensconced in an alcove all their own. The walls seemed like mullioned windows papered over with some sort of exotic film, and their mahogany table was so low that they had to kneel in order to sit. Floor cushions covered in colorful prints of pink floral trees and giant waves made it clear that this had been the decorator's intent.

Before the serving *geisha*—as Althorp termed it—left, they placed an order for two of the mysterious *sake* cups for Althorp and St. Cross and one pint of fine English stout for Lord Greenhope.

At Althorp's insistence, they each bent to remove their shoes inside their private little room, heightening the cultural correctness of the outing while also increasing the intimacy of the occasion. Stanley had never before removed his shoes in company, and—while he enjoyed distanced admiration from men who noticed his steel-cut and sapphire-crusted shoe buckles—he'd never felt any need to let others in on the secrets of his stockings nor of his shoe strap upkeep.

He was pleased to see that Althorp wore the same, traditional style of shoe, though his straps were more frayed and held together with engraved goldplate. St. Cross, on the other hand, straddled the line between gentry and adventurer, between male and female, and did so with great panache. Beneath her—*can I call her 'her' yet?*—staid black slacks, no one would ever know she wore knee-high boots.

He noticed Althorp also watching her deshodding with great interest. St. Cross rolled her trouser hems upward to reach the tops of her boots, just a few inches beneath the joint. Black, to match her regular gentlemanly attire, they laced in the old style common to peasants and to the pre-buckle days. The curved heel added two inches of height, slightly too much for a modern man, and copper rivets held the toe and heel leathers in place. At the instep and the shinguard, an extra strap reinforced the sturdiness of her practical footwear, attached by leaf-inspired buckles of a more artistic design than one usually saw in such multipurpose boots.

At a rhythmic patter of *click*ings and *whir*ings, Stanley gratefully redirected his attention to the table. It simply wouldn't do to be caught staring at a woman's feet—or a man's, either. On the smoothed and varnished tabletop, two dolls traversed from one side to the other. The dolls matched, from their bald heads with a key instead of a forelock to their geometric patterned robes under red shirts and flowery vests. In their hands, each held a plate with a bowl-like cup atop it.

By the time the dolls and cups reached Althorp and St. Cross, whose drinks must be on the little plates, the threesome had resumed their sitting positions. Althorp knelt on his cushion across from St. Cross, who sat on her hip, her knees off to one side and her top half in danger of falling against Stanley at any moment. Stanley sat stiffly beside her in the cross-legged fashion common to young boys and tailors.

St. Cross took her cup of gently warmed *sake*—it looked like weak, lukewarm tea to him, but Stanley couldn't fault her for testing the limits of new vogueries—and the serving doll bent its head, suddenly looking subservient rather than blank by the tilt of its posture. Firmly in the bowed position, it ceased moving entirely, standing politely in front of St. Cross, as if waiting for her to taste the brew and declare it acceptable or not.

Althorp took his own cup, paying less attention to the tiny machination which he'd surely seen before if he regularly haunted this place, and pledged a toast. "To missing!"

With a laugh, they clicked their glasses and cups together before taking hearty swigs. St. Cross fell to coughing immediately, and Althorp pounded her on the back. "It's not meant to be a single-swallow dram," he teased, even as he waved over the server and ordered her a second cup.

Stanley picked up one of the automatons. "However does this work?" he wondered aloud before starting to lift the elaborate layers of dressing.

"No!" Althorp cried.

As if reacting to the alarm in her second's voice, St. Cross wrapped her fingers around Stanley's wrist, arresting his motion towards the odd machine. Stanley stilled within her impossibly warm touch, feeling as though all the air in his lungs flowed through that circle of heat at the end of his arm.

Slowly, unwillingly, he twisted in her grasp. Immediately upon gaining his freedom, he missed the curl of her bones and the connection of their skins. A strangely loud silence fell over their quiet little table, and he'd no notion of how to outwardly react in order to smooth past the moment. After all, the three had never before spent much time together, and Stanley felt the awkward lack of conversation acutely. He'd no desire to discuss weather or other such innocuous topics with men he shared cards and life-and-death with. Yet, what else was there?

"It's impolite," Althorp explained, taking up the mantle of etiquette, "to look for the machinery. The Nipponese prefer the mystery and magic of a little man who serves your liquor."

The server reappeared, bowing much in the same manner as the dolls had done, before depositing two cups and a tiny pitcher of drink for them to share. Silently, the server cleared the table of dirty mugs and automatons, somewhat snidely ignoring the English-beer-drinking marquis.

Althorp poured a cup for the lady and then another for himself. "Slowly this time, old man." He demonstrated by taking a full sip, as though savoring a fine dry Madeira.

St. Cross mimicked the drinking style, and her eyes widened as she rolled the material through her mouth. Stanley couldn't help but find the bright eyes and pinking cheeks charming. Perhaps he shouldn't be party to heavy drinking with a woman, but St. Cross wasn't *really* a woman, for all her charms. Not if she'd attended and survived a duel. That made her one of the men, didn't it?

Somewhere in the midst of worrying about St. Cross's status, a discussion about the difference in gambling on cards rather than horses, and a shared fear of running afoul of the Patronesses of Almacks, they'd cracked a fourth bottle of *sake* and acquired quite a number of empty pint glasses.

"A pint of pure water's a pound and a quarter!" chirped Althorp.

But Stanley had a finer view of accounting with their neighbors across the pond. "A pint's a pound the world 'round," he countered.

St. Cross simply shook her head at both of them, possibly never having heard either of the mnemonics in her life in London. Come to think of it, other than being a poker player of some renown, where had St. Cross come from? Had she traveled the seas like Althorp? Been a lady of note in some genteel hideaway?

Stanley opened his mouth to ask, but found himself taking another slub of stout. A bit splashed to the table, and he hastily swiped it with his shirtsleeve. The laundress could fix the damage later. St. Cross was leaning heavily against Stanley's side now, her curly hair tickling his cheek and her spicy, linen scent filling his olfactory senses. He rather thought he ought to right her, but when he went to help her sit straight, he fell slightly against her shoulder in turn and had to catch himself on the table before going any further.

Good-humored Althorp, a true friend now, noticed their predicament and chuckled and cooed at the both of them. "Another pint," he called out to the serving staff, too loudly perhaps, but no one had yet moved to throw them out.

With only a slight stumble, Althorp rose from the table and bowed to the duelists in an attempt to act like he belonged. "Goodnight, gentlemen. I'm afraid my family gets nervous when they can't find me at this time of night, and you two are in no condition to drive yourselves anywhere. I must bid you *adieu.* Don't end your celebrations on my account." On his way out of their alcove, the viscount bumped into their returning server and oh-so-indiscreetly slipped it a note that must have been a decent size by the reaction. "My friends will need a place to sleep. Any chance they can stay in the assistant manager's rack tonight?"

The server bobbed like a buoy, and Althorp hurried off to wherever he was going.

"No, no," Stanley said to the serving *geisha*. "That's quite all right. We'll just take the barouche we arrived in after finishing this last round. No need for impropriety. I can certainly drive a horse or two."

When the server gently reminded him that the viscount had already made off with their only transportation, Stanley gave in to the inevitable. Nothing wrong with getting a bit foxed with a fellow and then sleeping it off. A bit juvenile, perhaps, but he'd done as much plenty of times in his youth.

He got an arm under St. Cross's shoulder. "Up you go." He lifted his drinking companion into a stumbling line and motioned to the server. "Lead on."

The server grabbed their footwear—one pair of sensible buckled and one pair of practical, but rather adventurous, riveted boots—and brought them to a wood-paneled side-room. It had one bed, a settee, and walls covered in scrolls depicting *koi* fish and characters that doubtless meant something to a man from the Orient, but not to Lord Greenhope.

The white-painted server closed the door on leaving, and Stanley noticed for the first time that he'd lost his sapphire-colored frock coat. Between that and the shoes, his attire leant itself easily to further trimming until sleep could be attained. Whyever had he thought to get dressed again and drive a team of horses?

St. Cross stumbled against the settee, moving it with a loud, scraping *swish*. She giggled as she bent over the curved arm, the shape of her back flowing into rounded buttocks and into thighs that molded themselves with the sloping furniture. His mouth went fuzzier at this forcible reminder of her womanhood. For surely no man had such flared hips and slender waist.

Her fingers fumbled on the tiny buttons of her starched white shirt, but she soon removed it to reveal a jacquard corset. Perhaps the corset would be considered slightly out of fashion for a woman, though demure enough to be eveningwear for even the most conservative lady. But on a man, it made an alluring surprise.

Yes, he'd known she cut a fine, womanish figure. And, yes, he'd known she wore a corset beneath her menswear, as if to remind herself and any who chose to notice that she observed all forms of propriety. But this! This secret gave him pause and made him feel at once out of sorts and proprietary. No one should get to see Mr. St. Cross in such vulnerable undergarments. Yet, could he deny the beauty of a lady in her luxe formalwear? Never.

He cleared his throat, trying not to look at her laced prettiness. "I don't believe I know your first name, St. Cross. Considering the day we've had..." *Yes, talk with her. Discuss something that has nothing to do with women or nakedness or sex.*

She tripped her way over to him, and he couldn't help but notice the way her corset ended over slim men's trousers. A conundrum. A juxtaposition. It made him long to see what hid beneath either piece of clothing, or both. He wanted to dress her in finery meant for either sex. Wanted to dress her in nothing at all. He needed to get some control over his wayward mind. It was the drink talking.

"Cara," she said, extending her hand in an inverted cup, like any woman would. "Cara St. Cross."

Gentility took over and merged with his desire to see her as a woman. He could no more have stopped himself from taking her hand and bending over it than he could have swum the Channel in December. "A pleasure, miss. My name is Stanley, though Lord Stanley and Lord Greenhope often suffice." *What am I even saying? She's got me all turned around with this closeness. Oh, God, Stanley, let go her hand.*

"Can you help me with this, Stanley?" she asked, turning around to present her laces. "I can't sleep in this boning."

Golden curls swirled at the nape of her neck, a neck tilted forward in perfect trust. With shaking hands, he reached for the silken cords, fussing with the knot in an attempt to avoid inhaling her scent or noticing the smoothness of her skin when accidentally brushed. Grommet by grommet, he pulled the ties from their would-be snares until he held a lanyard in one hand and the fabric of her corset with the other.

God could damn him for taking advantage later. Right now, he dropped the rope, unable to deny temptation any further. He parted the sides of her garment and kissed her naked back. With drink-softened lips, he pressed elasticity into the dents left by the bones and eyelets. She shivered beneath his mouth and made the quietest *mnh* noise in the back of her throat.

Emboldened by her response, sounds of gentle pleasure rather than admonishment, he slipped the bodice from her entirely, sliding his arms around her and soaking up her warmth while sucking on the sweat- and alcohol-slick side of her neck. She exhaled a light moan and leaned back into him. He couldn't help himself. He needed more. Needed to feel her, to taste her. To celebrate their lives and passions and togetherness.

He kissed his way up to suck her earlobe into his mouth, and she shuddered against him. She gave a little laugh, and he instinctively turned his head up just as she turned hers backwards.

Their lips met in an open, wet kiss. It was sloppy. It was sexual. It was glorious. Just a meeting of skin to skin, tongue to tongue, yet he felt it in his stomach, in his shoulders. In far earthier parts than they.

Knowing the ways of women, he let his hands drift upwards from her stomach, tracing patterns he longed to chase with tongue and eyes. Whorls of poetry written on each rib, and she arched in his arms languidly. He trailed his fingers over the slickly smooth outer edges of her breasts, and she gasped even as he pulled his hands away to make quick work of his own shirt and trousers.

With a whine, she turned to face him, and he paused in shedding his clothes to appreciate the fine art of her lines. The curve of a breast, the tautness of upper stomach, the curls on her head, the straight waistline of her trousers yet to be removed.

His hands were knocked away from their purpose, him all unwitting. She knelt at his feet with a sly smile and a mischievous tilt to her head. Her delicate fingers pulled at his unbuttoned frontfall and waist until the coverings puddled at his feet.

"Let me," she said, absolving him of any need to take control, to look out for her needs, to do anything other than enjoy this gift. And a good thing, too, since he wasn't sure he could, now that his blood had rushed all to one place and left good sense to be powered only by alcohol fumes.

Matching deeds to words, her hands came up to palm his buttocks, fingertips digging in strongly to massage and give him confidence in her strength and ability to hold him in place, hold him up when the time came. And then he had no more time to concentrate on her actions, for he was enveloped in hot, moist softness. Betimes, the pillowy aspect was broken by hard lines of sharp tooth—poignant, increasing his arousal further than he'd remembered its being before.

Soon, she sped him from firm and panting into desperation, her lips and sporadic teeth moving constantly over the mushroom head of his hardness. With the last of his cognizance, he kept himself from reaching out to crush her hair in his fists or smash her face against him. With a single yelp, he released his essence into her mouth, a lassitude washing over him that left him breathless and glad that her strong palms held him in place, for surely he'd fall without them.

He couldn't even complain when she spat his seed on the ground. His wife had never done this for him. Yet, here was a woman who'd fought for his honor and still had enough dignity of her own left to give this gift of mouth and luxury.

"In a moment," he breathed, knowing he couldn't leave her unsatisfied. Not after what she'd just done for him.

As gracefully as he could, he joined her in kneeling on the ground and reached for her trouser buttons, but again she batted him away.

"The apparatus is more than a little difficult," she explained, soothing the sting of rejection. "I can't take it off tonight."

Side by side on the floor, he leaned into her, feeling his muscles against her forgiving flesh. "But you don't need these." He plucked at the wool encasing her legs and then let her perform the removal. If the situation really did require her to keep on her metallic manhood, then he wouldn't get in the way of her wellbeing.

She blushed—as though she hadn't had his erection in her mouth!—and peeled out of her remaining clothing, revealing a trim warm body attached to a hard, silvery cock. Or was it the other way around? Strange that he couldn't look away, entranced by the sturdy inflexibility which had apparently been fastened into stiffness. It bore very little embellishment, strange in a woman whose other accessories had at least *some* detail, such as her naturalistic shoe buckles or her jacquard corset that no one ever saw. The lack of ornamentation made it seem less real somehow, not as much a part of her as it would be on a real man, even one who'd fashioned his own manhood.

"You deserve better."

He didn't know he'd cared about it until he said the words, but care he did. It wasn't right. She deserved to take pride in her cock as much as she did in any other detail of her appearance, of her identity. Foisted upon her or no, she'd accepted its presence, and this unadorned metal seemed a foreign object staked on.

Stanley reached out to touch, not the alien prick, but her outer thighs, reveling in her trembling. She may have been hiding it, but their taste of carnal delight had made her ready to die the little death in his arms. He glided across her skin, the suppleness of it and the gentle rifling of her hair guiding him to her inner thighs.

Her muscles tightened, but he stroked there, knowing what worried her. "Have no fear, *Cara mia.* I won't try to move your shaft this night."

It took a moment more of soothing caresses, but then she relaxed beside him, letting him turn her to her hands and knees.

"This canvas, I am allowed to work with." It was half question, half statement, and she answered it clearly with a quiet whine as he smoothed her vertebrae.

Up and down, side to side, he teased and brushed her spine, nuzzled and massaged, till she fairly vibrated beneath him. He worked lower and lower till he could nip at her rear and smell the earthy Cara-ness that tantalized him more than even her simple glycerin soap. She jumped right into his molding hands when he flicked his tongue against her dark orifice, and he grinned into her crease, having known that this would be her response, that the sensitive nerves there would only heighten the feeling.

More firmly now, he pulled apart the roundedness of her cheeks to delve in more deeply, loving every loud moan she couldn't contain. Licking the outside and then tapping at the rim of the muscle until it began to expand and contract in its own rhythm, he brought her to higher plains of pleasure. Waiting for the right moment, for the time when the gasps and the desires ran wild and he could join her in passion once again.

"More!" she cried out, head falling to meet the floor with a quiet thump.

Yes, she was ready. He spat into his hand a few times and smeared the only lubrication available onto his virile member. Then slowly, oh, achingly slowly, he circled it where his tongue had been, letting her get used to the new texture and size, letting her know what was to come.

His patience was cut short when she pushed herself back with a loud, inarticulate cry, forcing him into her as deeply as he'd ever hoped she'd allow. One of his hands rested on her hip, trying to guide her movements, but the other was captured by his new lover. She pulled it—and him—forward, demanding by example that he smooth the side of her breast, repeating the motion till rawness or intensity demanded he choose a new location for the rasping pet.

By the time he'd worked his way from outer edge of the breast to sensitive skin beside the aureole, she was screaming and writhing and working herself onto his shaft with complete abandon. So close, she was so close. And, suddenly, he realized, so was he. He'd been so caught up in her needs and her beauty that he'd ignored his own.

But now he could feel his body tightening and his muscles shaking and his need to drive, drive, drive on to the peak that lay within reach. With two flicks of his thumb across her attentive nipple, she wailed out her release and her sphincter tightened around him, prompting his own *petite mort.*

He barely had the energy to pull out and curl around her before they both fell into a dreamless, soused sleep.

CHAPTER THREE – DAVID MCALPINE

Back at the St. Cross townhouse, all was quiet... just the way David McAlpine hoped to find it. *That cove won't get away with stealin' my money!* He aimed to take back every bit the bastard had cheated away. And then some. Clearly the bloke did all right for himself, and wouldn't mind a bit of silver going missing.

McAlpine had never broken into a building before, but you heard about its happening all the time out there in the big city. *Here* in the big city, that was. So it couldn't be all that impossible. Right?

The streetlights' luminous strands didn't reach around the side of the house at Shaftesbury Square. Just to be sure, he climbed the curlicues of a wrought-iron stand and punched the large globe at the apex.

"Damnation!" he screeched as hot carbon gas enveloped his fist and shards of glass punctured his skin. He fell from the thermolampe with a *thump*, then scuffled off to the hedges next to his townhouse objective.

Barely in time, too. The door of another rich man's mansion opened, and a cultured voice called out, "I say there! Does anyone need some help? We can send for a doctor."

The posh lackey stood silhouetted in the night, breathing through that nasal accent and flapping his tail-coat in the evening breeze. McAlpine pressed himself against the bricks and waited for the danger to pass. In only a few moments, the false creature grew bored and withdrew back into his luxurious slavery.

McAlpine heaved a sigh of relief, then gasped and held that breath. *Did anyone hear me? Are those the footsteps of someone coming to check the street, to make sure no one intends to rob him blind?*

Fuck. Thieving was hard. And he hadn't even got inside yet.

But not to give up. Not to act like a sow running from the wolf that wanted to eat her babies. Not to cower from some gallied sot who meant to scare him off from what was rightfully his.

That bloody St. Cross! The varmint had cleaned him out, and when he could ill afford it with the harvest fresh over from a bad year and his drinking debts piling up. McAlpine could scarce afford to be here in London instead of home on the farm, working like honest folk, but St. Cross had stolen his means and then run away. Run away like a tender upstart who couldn't stomach the real life in the countryside and couldn't handle the men who wanted to take back what was theirs.

He checked the street one more time, but saw no new lanterns come fresh to the walkways. Standing from his hedgerow crouch, he tugged on his brown coat, brushing the dirt from the sleeves—though not bothering with the elbows—and emerging into the empty lane. Calm as you please, like he was meant to be there, McAlpine turned from the road and walked the dark side of the house, tracing his fingers along the bricking.

"Ow!" he cried as his coatsleeve got stuck by a thorn. While it did not actually pierce him, the pricking came as a surprise.

He threw himself at the ground posthaste, acquiring scrapes and bumps, listening carefully for any urchin who might have heard his dismay and come to find out the matter. Nothing. Silence. He breathed the dirt for a few more moments, then righted himself once again.

"Listen here, David McAlpine," he whispered to himself. "No more of this mucky mouth. Keep yourself quiet and get the blunt what he owes you."

For the troth this time, he crept towards the back of the house and scaled the back wall to the dark window, catlike as you please. *No mouser trained by a barn full of wary, Italian mice has anything on David McAlpine.*

Of course, making the pane was easy, but then he had to get through it. With the hand already full of shards, he struck out. His knuckles bounced off the leaded glass, driving home the fragmented splinters-in-residence.

"Gyaaash—!"

He bit back the howl of pain. This time, however, the damage could not be undone. Had not gone unnoticed.

Lights glowed within the townhouse, and a man's voice called out. "Ho, there!" By the timbre and volume, the home's protector had to be six foot at least, and burly like a draught horse.

Rabbit-quick, he rolled off the ledge, *thump*ing for the last time upon the ground. *No more, St. Cross. You'll not hurt me any more.*

A great clamor rose from the house now, as more people awakened and stampeded to the doors, lanterns and muskets and swords in hand. Not that McAlpine could see them, but he knew they were coming. They thought they'd be agents of property and law, but did they know St. Cross had taken his money? Did they? Would they defend that cub then?

Not wanting to loiter for a beating or for explanations, he vacated into the night. After this disappointment, he needed a bracing fine drink.

* * *

McAlpine wrapped his abused hand around his eighth quart of brown ale, mindlessly using the other to play with splinters from the bar. Would it never end? Would he be persecuted by these city fops and their dishonest ways forever?

He only wanted his own swindled goods. Was it too much to ask? *Oooh, look at the line of white around the rim of this glass...* Caught up in his beer and his misery, McAlpine didn't notice when a man took the stool beside him.

"He's not done right by you, ay?" the man asked in a fantastic accent that had no nation, no district, and was obviously put on.

McAlpine didn't care much about the accent one way or the other and wanted to send the surpriser away. Still, how did this odd gent know all about St. Cross's deceptive guile?

The stranger waved down the publican. "How about something other than taplash for my new friend?" he requested.

McAlpine had been perfectly happy with his beer, not finding it at all thick or bottomy, but who was he to naysay a free pint? It was free, right?

"Don't trouble, my fine man. I'll catch the account for this one." The newcomer tipped his own drink in drunkards' camaraderie. His was of a paler color and already half empty. "You've a problem, ay?"

And at this slight provocation, McAlpine found himself telling the man—named Geoffrey Black—all about that devil St. Cross and all his bloody clods of money, taken unfairly and untimely from honest folk who only meant to play a hand or two before heading home. Black nodded in all the right places and asked all the right questions... and put all the right pints in front of him at compliments.

Drink after drink, the lot of it came out till the country man found himself in tears over the splintering bar, describing how St. Cross sliced his small savings away, one game at a time. Black patted at his shoulder, all sympathy, and filled his ears with confirmation. Oh, yes, the card-sharp was a vile lout, no fellow feeling, bound to get his in the end.

And wouldn't McAlpine like, Black asked, to be involved in making sure that St. Cross got his desserts, ay?

Aye.

CHAPTER FOUR – CARA

Cara woke to a dual throbbing in her head and her nether regions. Memories of excessive drinking could explain both.

She had to wonder whether she could get away with waiting to relieve herself until after the removal of her metal appendage. The pounding of her bladder dashed the wish, and she could only hope one ill-formed night wouldn't lead to infections and further discomfort.

She pushed herself up with one hand and froze, partially from her spinning head. And partially because she didn't know her location. This couch wasn't upholstered in her serviceable calico, nor was it empty. Her bare arm looked markedly pale in contrast to the tanned one it leaned against, and Cara didn't want to look up and follow that darker limb to its owner.

But she had to know. Last she recalled, she'd gone for a kip with Althorp and Greenhope, two gentlemen of breeding and good standing. If she'd lain with one of them... the consequences could be dire. As members of the Club, they'd both heretofore been too well bred to notice her lack of manly accoutrements. Such intimacy would force the issue, leading to discomfort, friction, and an ending to her comfortable life.

She'd walked the fine line between *accepted aristo-male* and *lower-city sideshow* for weeks now, and she'd prefer to continue. But if she'd had sex, if one of them had seen her as a woman, then he would be bound to treat her as such or tear himself apart trying not to. For, surely, he could no more treat her as a man than he did any other mistress.

Then again, she'd technically done nothing a man couldn't, or so the continued wearing of her cock and the soreness in her rump informed her. *So he can make you his catamite rather than his woman?* The idea didn't suit, but it might not be as awful. No, it wouldn't be as awful if she'd truly been an uppercrust gentleman, but one whiff of scandal would send her straight back down where they'd all tell themselves she'd always belonged.

No more putting it off, her urinary tract told her. Cara looked up into the pale face and dark eyes of Stanley, Lord Greenhope. His shaking fingers and horrified O of a mouth told her everything she needed. She could still salvage the situation.

"We must never speak of this again," she said sternly, firmly meeting his gaze and willing him to cave to her demand.

He nodded, a small tilting bob of the chin. "No, no. Quite right. A simple accident and affair of too much drink." He blanched further at *affair.* "That is to say..." He twisted his hands helplessly around the idea of their togetherness.

She stood in a strong, controlled motion, not letting him see a wince because of her headache or bladder. She had to be collected, elegant. Had to convince him that she was masculine in all the regular senses and that her de-sires should be obeyed. However he chose to act this morning, it would forever paint their associations.

She tossed him his shirt, finding her own shirt and corset underneath it. Could she ask him to lace her up? No, he didn't need the reminder, neither of her femininity nor of the previous night's unlacing. She'd be taking a carriage home anyway.

In silence, she garbed herself, watching from the corner of her eye as his muscled chest and shapely thighs were swathed and hidden by his own raiment. With a very posh nod of satisfaction at their proper appearances, she found the proprietor of the establishment and had him send for a barouche. In the meanwhile, she intended to use the chamber pot, far from the prying eyes of any others.

* * *

Over the next week, Cara noticed that Greenhope, not previously keen, made himself a regular at the poker table. Every night, he'd join the game. And, by Saturday, he had a regular seat and a regular color, the sapphire chips staying untouched on the gaming racks, unarguably his.

He'd only sat in once or twice before in the whole time she'd been a member, but since that fateful night—which she was *not* speaking of, not even in her own head—he'd become a staple. He played a decent game, passive but passably tight, though nowhere near her or Althorp's league.

And did Althorp know what had gone on at the Nipponese bar? No, no, he mustn't. He'd not looked at her and Greenhope any differently than he had prior to that night. Had not treated her in any strange ways, other than to extend an invitation to test her newfound mettle against the Tower's crows.

This evening, Greenhope sat beside her, as he'd done every night this week. His freshly laundered shirt smelled of sharp lime and was a bit thin, thin enough for her to see the outline of his bicep and remember how it had felt, locked around her middle, holding her close.

Oh, yes, in the days gone, she'd remembered all the events of that fateful encounter, the alcoholic glaze retreating into crisp reality. But while she might keep herself a bit warm, alone and in bed, with the memory of his powerful form harnessed to her will or with the still-tender bruises on her hips, she might also live in fear of anything's changing.

And change it had already. For what was Greenhope doing, sitting so sanguine beside her? Demanding her attention with his simple existence?

"So, St. Cross," began Greenhope as he checked a bet, "we all know you're a remarkable poker master." At this, Althorp called *hear, hear!*; the earl grum-bled; and the man in the fifth seat nodded. "You must tell us how you first took up the game."

Curse you, Greenhope. She didn't want to talk, to remind them of her humble beginnings or womanish nature. What was more, she could see this for the thin ploy it was. The end had come to her gentle charade; now it had only its death throes to complete. Greenhope wanted to *know* her—Cara, not St. Cross—and that game shouldn't float.

Her answer came curt and uninformative, nothing they couldn't guess. Damned if she'd help them send her down. "I learned the sport as a child, discovered some aptitude for it, and pursued the skill at gatherings of ever-increasing stakes." And that was all she'd say on the matter.

The earl saved her from causing a discourteous scene. He let out a rueful sound. "And to my misfortune, he's come to join us." But the dramatic delivery belied the words and spread a warm camaraderie through the gathering.

Cara felt a shiver of not-fear. Not precisely. When before had she belonged to such a circle of like-minded others? Ones who accepted all she had to offer—from talents to aspirations? Yet, even for that, they didn't accept *all* of her.

Aye, there's the rub. Somehow, pretending to be fundamentally what she wasn't—male, aristocrat—gave her more a sense of self than ever before. Now that she came so close to losing it all, she knew she had to grasp at this life and identity with her strength entire. What meant masculine or feminine, noble or commoner? Labels. Transport. They meant nothing in the face of poker and loyalty, of understanding and companionship.

"Perhaps," suggested Althorp, "St. Cross would lead us on a trip to visit the world's best gaming houses."

Warm, accepted, belonging, Cara shook her head and raised the bet. "This, gentlemen, is by far the best establishment I have ever had the good fortune to attend. One of us would have to build another to make the leaving worthwhile."

"Hear, hear!" agreed the earl, who perhaps knew better than the rest the sort of houses St. Cross could guide them through, not at all appropriate even for a lord accustomed to barbaric travels.

General consensus filled the table. Then cards shuffled and chips changed owners well into the night.

* * *

Having collected her promissory and tender notes from the gracious losers, Cara racked up her chips and began to tidy the card room. She knew she needn't bother, knew she might leave the task for the help, but it made a good excuse to have the room to herself. While the other players smoked and drank their way into the foyer or the study, she kept company with the silent calm of the cards and chips.

Well, usually that made the whole room. Tonight, she also had Althorp. He'd lingered at the table, waving off conversational gambits from others and watching amber liquid slant along the sides of his glass.

Yes, Althorp did often spend extra time in her presence, their having struck up a fast friendship, but never while being so quiet, nor so fidgety. She couldn't take it anymore. "Out with it, then," she said, her voice impatient but not unkind.

"Is there something bothering you, Crossy?" he asked. "Whatever it is, you must know by now that I'll stand your friend."

She felt a surge of happiness at the nickname. Good enough that Althorp had never called her ought besides *St. Cross* or *old man*, but to receive a boyish naming like this! He necessarily saw her not only as a social equal, but also as a close friend, one whom he had the right to name.

But she couldn't tell him about the debacle with Greenhope. She'd be forever tainted with a feminine nature in his eyes, eyes that beheld her now with all the solidarity she'd never known she wanted. Why couldn't she have been born *Mister* St. Cross? Better yet, *Lord* St. Cross. Everything that she'd done since joining this rarefied society had brought her closer to that pinnacle of self-satisfaction everyone hoped for but few ever attained.

So, sex with Greenhope was out of bounds. The bizarre other events of that evening, however, were not. "Someone tried to break into my townhouse the night of the duel," she chose to tell him. At his look of alarm, she hastened to reassure, "Nothing was taken. My doorman ran him off."

"Your doorman?" Althorp tilted his head quizzically, then his eyes went comically wide in memory. "You can't possibly mean that slip of a boy."

"Quite prodigious, isn't he? Sending a grown man scuttling off before his youthful might."

Althorp shook his head, willing to share the merriment with her, except, "And *that's* what has you so dashed rattled?"

Preferring to offer up this worry in place of the other, she let him draw her out. "I have to wonder how a man could infiltrate my street and get so far as shattering a kitchen window before the citizenry took notice of him." She took heart in his encouraging nod. "And now I find myself flustered at the oddest times, unsure whether any street is safe, whether I can trust the steadfastness of my walls. And... I often think I see the same beaten-up cab following me around London."

It was silly. She knew it was. A botched break-in didn't make her the target of some criminal's unfulfilled vendetta. Other houses on the street surely offered more thrill and interest. Hers had simply been the lucky, convenient one. Nothing suggested premeditation on the thief's part, and yet she couldn't shake the feeling of being followed, of being hated with such virulent purpose as to make even visiting the club into an ordeal fraught with peril.

Althorp pushed back from the table and crossed to the chip rack in order to give her a hearty clap on the shoulder. "We'll all keep an eye out for suspicious miscreants," he jollied her. "If any one dares to follow the Caller Club's Mister St. Cross, then he'll be drummed out of London posthaste. And possibly with a few broken bones."

The door opened, and Greenhope entered, attention immediately focused on Cara. "Ah, St. Cross, there you are. I'd hoped for a moment of your time."

Althorp cleared his throat pointedly, and the marquis nodded his way, all apologetic poise.

"Good to see you, Althorp," greeted the new arrival. "I trust you're well."

Courtesy successfully observed, Althorp bowed to both of them, the barest tilt of upper body. It didn't even move his hair. "Likewise, Greenhope. If the two of you will excuse me, I have other matters to attend." With that polite vaguery, the viscount took his leave.

Cara watched Greenhope—she refused to think of him as *Stanley*; they could still recover from their slip a week gone if only they took care to practice circumspection—as closely as she would a man who'd both been on a winning streak and wore a bulky sack coat. "You played well this evening," she opened the conversation, trying to keep him on innocuous topics from the start.

He bobbed his head vigorously, as though grateful for the gambit, for all that he must have had some purpose in seeking her company. "Thank you. That's quite the compliment from your mouth." His gaze dipped to her lips as he spoke the final word.

She sent her tongue out to moisten them, suddenly dry under his regard, her own eyes helplessly drawn to his comparative part. In their kisses, he'd moved his tongue with such skill, drawn her into his seductive web with the subtle movements and sensual strokes. Was it drunken talent, or would he feel equally as good now, sober and scared? She wanted to reach out and grab his neck, to force him down to her level, and she barely held herself in check.

"Confound it!" he cried, slamming a powerful fist against the much-abused card table. "There's no reason we shouldn't take public joy in each other's company. We're both men of the Caller. We can be seen together drinking or gambling."

They left unsaid their joint feelings of uneasiness. There was no reason they shouldn't do those things, and yet Cara knew by his speech that Greenhope too felt threatened and nervous by their physical proximity. How easily their closeness could transform into something far more dangerous to reputation and honor.

She wouldn't be the one to admit such a fear, though, not now that Greenhope had pointed out its basis in supposed fiction. "Would you have a drink with me?" she invited him, perhaps foolishly, because even though the anxiety must go unvoiced, she still acknowledged it inside of her soul. She hadn't got this far in life by lying to herself.

Determined to show off their manly camaraderie and unaffectedness, they shouted for a cabriolet to be brought round and announced their intent to go for a drink at the Three Goats in Chelsea. None joined them, a blessing since the cab only seated two if they squished.

So, they squished. Leg to leg, bicep to bicep. The swaying of the cab knocked them into each other—politely ignored—and into the paisley upholstery. Cara's jacket stuck to the leather seats, somehow overwarm on this chilly November night.

"Lovely evening," said Lord Greenhope, turning to face her.

The move succeeded in knocking their knees together obscenely—if she'd been a lady—and giving her the chance to smell his puffing breath. She breathed deep of his brandy-scented speech, letting the residual alcohol send tingles through her nose and into her throat, down into her lungs and along the passageways into her breasts, setting them to a tightening excitement. That was only a reaction to the alcohol. Nothing more.

"Quite," she agreed. Then she turned away, looking out the window and angling her knees doorward so that they no longer smacked together with his or forced an inappropriate closeness. Of course, the window was covered over with a black velvet curtain, but this made a small obstacle and could be easily remedied whenever she desired. *Hmm. The velvet appears to have a worn patch just below eye-height.*

She paid a studied inattention to her cab mate, waiting for the stuffy confinement to let them go to rejoin the world. Lord Greenhope's hand appeared in her peripheral vision, tapered fingers fluttering in midair and then falling out of her sight to land with a disheartened thump. She didn't look to see where they'd ended up. *Nothing to see here.* Damn, but she couldn't breathe. They'd sucked up all the air in the cab until nothing remained other than heat and sweat and a refusal to gasp.

Finally, the vehicle rolled to a stop. Cara didn't wait for the driver to leap down and set out a step. Didn't make sure that they'd come to the terminus instead of just pausing for a passel of nightschool children or blinded whores. She slid back the latch and threw the door; it bounced on the black metal of the frame and came right back at her but was arrested by her foot nudging it back towards the obtuse position. The driver shrieked at the clanging.

She lit down to the cobbled street and filled her senses with cool humidity. Any other time, she'd be hunting for the cloak she'd left at the Club. Tonight, the breeze ran over her form, pushing through her clothing to writhe against her skin in a lover's caress. Arms spread wide to gather as much freedom as she could, she lifted her face upwards into the wind. Her blonde curls ruffled, wild in the night.

Stillness at her back, a windbreak if she chose to use it. "Shall we?" she asked the block without looking to be sure it answered to *Stanley, Lord Greenhope.* And she led him into the well-lit pub, feeling its commonness with every step.

Well, if he'd wanted to stay in his aristocratic balloon, he'd never have come out to merge with the rabble here, not that the denizens of Chelsea counted as rabble. She, of course, could only stay on the more *tonnish* sides of town. Anywhere else, they'd toss her out until she returned in proper attire. Her reputation among the upper crust gave her plenty of leeway in certain areas of London, but it also made her a dangerous target in other sections.

They acquired some of the new India Pale Ale at the bar before staking out a small, round table at a hidden window, nestled between an interior wall and a rowdy group of students. They shared the hard wooden bench, side by side, overlooking the street, which was mostly empty save for vehicles rattling onto other places.

"A bit class," Greenhope remarked.

Cara looked around them and couldn't help but agree. The clean floors, the polished tables, the broken-in but not broken-up furniture all pointed in that direction. Still, Greenhope couldn't possibly be the pub-going type, not even in Chelsea. He had drawing rooms and clubs, balls and calling occasions. "Depends what you compare it against."

Greenhope took a deep drink, half the pint in one draft. "There was this one bar in Tortuga," he confided. "Lord above! The floor splintered when you walked on it, and the beer was shark piss. 'Course, those were the good parts. The clientele? Well..." His hands spread wide to demonstrate the helplessness of it.

"When were you in Tortuga?" And she'd worried they'd have nothing to discuss. But here sat her former lover, telling such interesting stories. Other than Althorp, who'd traveled in the Navy, she didn't think of the upper crust as people who moved about much. Going from townhouses to country houses with nary a meaningful excursion in between to break the monotony, more like.

"Ah, I was a young man, then, not yet Marquis of Greenhope, but just a courtesy baron. My grandfather railed long and hard about my going into any sort of *trade*. You know how it is." He paused to let her nod, though she certainly didn't know how it was. Trade had always seemed so respectable to her. "I tried to pacify him by explaining that I was going to acquire new lands for the family to manage, to make him Duke of New Greenhope or what have you." He tossed back the rest of his glass. "You dry?"

To match him, she finished her own pint as he stood up. Moments later, he came back with another round of India Pale for both of them, and she could see the publican sipping his own dark porter.

"Ah, New Greenhope." He picked up the thread of his story again. "Well, if I was going to make that argument, I needed to go out and survey my lands-to-be, not that I'd made any progress on that score since it hadn't been my actual purpose. I'd wanted to get into the import-export business, bringing goods from all over the Empire into our little corner of London, being the man who had everything or knew where to get it, no matter how exotic."

She could envision him as a boy, all bright eyed and excited over Dutch china or Chinese lacquer boxes. Had he wanted to ride elephants in India or hunt for ivory in Africa?

"I'd been getting outlandish repair bills from a ship-yard in Tortuga with nothing in the descriptions to explain the costs. So I told grandfather that I needed to see if there were any estates worth claiming in the Indies, and jumped on one of my own ships headed west." He leaned close and lowered his voice. "Turned out, the shipyard didn't do much work at all, but sold the best rumbullion for miles around."

"No! They didn't." She shook her head and took a drink.

He laid an arm around her shoulders, friendly. "They'd been tacking the liquor ration onto the upkeep costs for months."

How exciting! "What did you do?" she asked breath-lessly, watching his pupils darken and expand.

"Bought some more rum, of course. A good ship owner trusts his officers."

She tipped back her glass, surprised to find it empty, and briefly took her leave to buy the next round. When she came back, she slid onto the bench beside him, re-suming their close position intended for punch lines. His hand returned to her shoulder, as well it should. They needed to get back into their posture to continue the evening.

"That sounds marvelous," she said, not caring for the genteel womanishness of her phrasing. "Whyever did you stop taking such trips?"

Stanley shrugged, a strangely lower-class gesture that seemed out of place on this man. Airily, he replied, "When I became Marquis of Greenhope, I couldn't go gallivanting off around the world anymore. I had to protect the family's interests here in England, be part of Her Majesty's loyal retainership, and so on. If I had an heir or two, perhaps the situation would be different."

She covered his hand on the table with her own. "I've never left the Isles at all," she volunteered, "so you're ahead of me." Her fingers stroked along the back of his hand, sateen and velvet underneath the tips sending warm jolts up through her bones.

Stanley excused himself for a moment and returned with four pints, spilling some of the golden liquid onto the table as he set them down. Drinks delivered, he sat on the bench and scooted across till they were once again side by side, his arm around her shoulders and her hand upon his hand. This time, with all the arranging of limbs, Cara couldn't help but notice the situational oddness. She'd never seen two men out having lark who made sure to entwine their bodies this way. She'd never been quite so interested in staring into a man's eyes while he told her about himself.

Giving herself a moment to think, she tore her gaze from his beautiful brown eyes, so rich and deep, and back to the scratched glasses. She brought a pint to her lips and sipped delicately, trying to keep from actually drinking, to clear her head. Even when purposely *not* making time, she and Greenhope fell into this flirtatious trap. They could end up sharing intimacies again so easily. She'd have to find a way to take control of the situation. She wouldn't be made an unsuitable poker player.

"But you've been all over the Isles," Stanley said, as though that rivaled sailing to Tortuga. "I believe the earl lost a hand to you all the way in Belfast."

With a vague smile, she told him all about playing her way across the country, seeking out rarer and rarer games and targeting the earl the moment she'd recognized him. She used voices, and he laughed in all the right places, but he only had half her attention. No, a quarter of it. A quarter of her attention on a story she could've told while figuring odds from a seven-card game.

That left a quarter of her attention on the rising desire to press fully against him, instead of staying in this too-loose-too-tight half-embrace. And half her attention determined to work this out to her advantage, or at least to her minimal detriment.

From the posture and the warmth, she'd bet on their finishing the evening in a compromising situation again. But she could work with this. She could keep her man and her own weaknesses from gaining power over her, could possibly even work the odds so that she came out ahead.

"Greenhope," she interrupted herself. If he cared to hear more, she could recreate the story of her first and last attempt at dice over cards later. "It's getting late. Would you care to join me for a nightcap?"

His mouth opened and closed a few times, though he didn't move his arm nor his hand. So, how would he fall? Was it an inappropriate proposition, a drink between friends, or something more?

He rotated the hand underneath hers so that they pressed palm to palm in intimate accord. "I'd like nothing better."

* * *

She barreled through the front doors of the Shaftesbury Square residence, Lord Greenhope in her wake. "Nathan!" she called her butler-manservant-cook. "Anything to report?"

The former urchin popped into the foyer and trailed her as she climbed the stairs. "Nothing amiss, ma'am."

Oh, thank God. With the imperious wave that he'd

helped her practice, she dismissed him and told him to send Mindy along. At least she wouldn't have to tell Greenhope about the attempted robbery and her subsequent uneasiness. If she was right, if some blackguard had been following her, the townhouse was no less safe than anywhere else. And if she was wrong, then it didn't matter.

Not hearing any other steps on her stairs, Cara checked that her lover—just as eager as she, only moments ago—still followed. Silly man. He remained at the foot of the case, hands stuffed into his pockets and casting about with a confused eye for anyone to take his things or give him some direction.

"Come along, then," she beckoned from her spot, meeting his eyes and holding his gaze till he looked down. "This way."

Without protest, he climbed the rise behind her and let her deposit him in her bedroom. She refused to think of it as shabby, the worn paisley at odds with his perfectly pressed silk-wool trousers and brightly polished pocketwatch strapped to his wrist with tooled leather and lashed-on measurement devices.

"Disrobe for me," she commanded.

He balked, sinking to sit on the bed in his surprise. *Not the perfect man, then.* Well, fine. She could make this easy for him. Get him used to the idea of taking orders from her. So long as she kept control of their encounter, his behavior needn't outwardly change. Besides, here was her chance to play the bravura.

"You can fold your things over that chair." She pointed to a piece of furniture at her vanity, as though he hadn't just disobeyed, as though she hadn't shocked him even through his arousal. "I need to change into something more feminine."

Ah, there was the look she needed. His eyes lit at the very idea, and he flipped his collar to remove both it and his tie. If she looked down, she was sure she'd see other evidence of his renewed interest, but that would be far too forward and impolite.

Sure that he'd follow her instructions this time, she let herself out, meeting with Mindy in the hallway. Mindy whisked her off to the girl's own room. It would serve as a dressing room since her own boudoir had been appropriated by her evening's entertainment.

"I found some of your prettier things in an unopened trunk you sent from Belfast," Mindy said as she efficiently stripped off Cara's outer garments. She paused on the buckles of her masculinity holster. "Unless you want to do this as a man?"

Cara shook her head. No, she'd go to him as a woman. Assert her power and... oh, who was she trying to fool? A gorgeous, naked man waited on her bed for her return, and she wanted to experience him as herself. As Cara. Not the fictional *Mister St. Cross.*

Reassured by whatever look must have crossed Cara's face, Mindy resumed her tasks. As painlessly as possible, she removed the penile apparatus and ran a washcloth over the sweaty pools it had created. Finally, she brought out a green silk nightgown. She stood on a chair to get it over Cara's head, then smoothed the bunches of fabric till it hung in soft folds to the floor.

The silk felt cozy and sensual at once, like flickering gazes from interested strangers or like a wool sweater lined with a well-worn blanket. Mindy slipped a short kimono of the same green over the peignoir, tying it with two belts arranged in complimentary bows over her hipbones.

Cara looked at herself in the mirror. Nearly naked in this eveningwear that enticed with tactility where it didn't show off her figure, blonde curls brushed to fall free around her ears, she looked more feminine than she had in months. She pointed a toe, and watched her reflection do the same. With a loud breath, she relaxed her shoulders and smiled at the odd beauty in the looking glass.

For tonight, only tonight, she didn't have to pretend anymore.

"Have fun!" Mindy called with a teenager's prurient interest as Cara walked out the door.

She intended to. And the posed tableau that greeted her when she slid into her bedroom made her think that *fun* would be the least of the adjectives available by the time the night ended. Greenhope had lit all of her candles, their flickering lights casting shadows and patches full of soft lumens at random. He'd also found her one electric lamp and cranked its battery to provide a warm, modern glow that radiated out from the foot of the bed. Lying stretched out on her duvet, all smooth planes and intriguing pale-to-tan delineations, Greenhope watched the door with hunter's eyes. He tracked her movements as she entered, stalked her with his gaze as she drew nearer and skirted a candelabrum or two.

"*Cara mia*," he choked in a strangled whisper. "So beautiful. Did you dress for me?"

What a sweet man; she wouldn't point out the ridiculousness of his question. He obviously had gone to quite a bit of effort to set up the right mood and make himself exceedingly desirable, but he'd not expected her to do the same on his behalf. Did his cheating wife treat him so badly that he'd learned to do nothing but give during a sexual encounter? Well, she could change that, could reward him for his efforts and his eagerness to please.

She slunk towards him till she stood at the side of the bed, pleased to see that he didn't move from his position. He'd lain himself out for her, a naked feast for her eyes, and it gladdened her that he wouldn't revoke the gift in his craving to touch.

Achingly slowly, she pulled the strings of one sash, the bow shrinking, shrinking to nothing, then coming undone, leaving a strip of silk in her hand. His breathing sped and his pupils dilated, fixed on the green tie. Now she moved to the second bow, pulling again slowly. At half size, she stopped and took her hands from her waist.

Stanley moaned quietly, eyes still locked on the bow and reaching out, as if compelled, to complete the action. Cara caught his wrist, as she'd done that night when they'd drunk themselves into curiosity.

"Shh," she whispered. Her fingers trailed from his wrist to his elbow, and she joined him on the duvet to press his arm above his head. She stroked the underside of his upper arm, and he shivered at the light touch in a place no one ever saw. "Let me."

He gave her a quizzical look, partially pulled from his voyeuristic haze, but the look cleared when she twined the first silk tie around his wrist. A quick nod and a swallow gave her all the permission she needed. Loop upon loop, to be sure of the hold, she attached him to her wooden headboard. Loop upon loop, he relaxed into her mattress. Yes, this was what they both needed. He could give up control, give up all his concerns and worries. She, on the other hand, would gain her position and her pleasure, and she could make this so good for him.

She readjusted herself to straddle his waist, too high for him to get any sort of thrustable friction, but perfectly placed for the back of her silk jacket to brush him like the backs of a thousand well-manicured hands. Now she resumed the untying of the second bow, and when his eyes and hand both followed her movement, she knew it for the playful test it was.

Again, she caught his wrist, and he grinned at her unrepentantly. Well, if he wanted to be shown his place, she'd give it to him. No more slow and teasing. She'd take him straight from sensation to perfection and demonstrate who was in charge in her bed. More strongly now, using muscles worked in sword practice, she pushed this second arm above his head, letting her torso hang low over his face, kimono falling open to reveal milk-pale skin and the low-cut gown beneath.

He strained upward to press his mouth to her skin, but couldn't move far enough to get more than a mouthful of draping silk. She laughed, low and easy, as she tied him more securely to her bed, reveling in the feel of him between her legs, in his obvious desire for her body.

"Trust me to take care of you," she said, half breathy sexuality and half command.

He writhed briefly in his bonds, testing them, then lay unmoving, staring up at her with blown pupils and a slackly surprised need on his face. "Please," he begged, unable to articulate more than that.

She shrugged out of the kimono jacket, leaving only the long gown that bared her arms and most of her chest, but still covered the rest with brushing tantalization. "I know what you need."

She'd have to take care of his current arousal quickly. She could already tell that he was too far gone to last. The almost mechanical-sounding whines that she pulled from his throat by the mere brush of her mouth or gown told her enough. Told her he'd never been set free from expectations this way.

She wouldn't torture him. As she shimmied downwards, she dropped kisses along the muscled lines of his chest and stomach, flicking a tongue into his navel, which made him cry out and arch upwards. Cara put strong, steadying hands on his hips, both a reminder and a vice that wouldn't let him buck again. He moaned, long and high pitched, at her restraint, growing impossibly harder underneath her chin, but he didn't try to twist out of her grip.

"Good boy." With that, she closed her lips around the head of his penis and ran her tongue over the tip.

He screamed, but didn't move, and she smiled around her treat, imagining the look on his face—twisted in a rictus of ecstasy—and his hands clenching futilely on the ties or the thick, wooden slats above his head. Did she hear a shaking and pulling from that end?

Going straight to what he needed, she bobbed up and down on his cock, hot and full in her mouth. She made sure to drag at the flap of skin that marked transition to glans from shaft with her lips every time she came up, then tightened her lips on the way down. Faster and faster she moved, wringing moans of pleasure and twitches of desperate, unconscious movement from him. When she attempted a scrape of the teeth along his sensitive rod, he exploded into her mouth and she held him there, milking him through all the aftershocks.

When she was sure he'd spent himself fully, Cara let go his pelvis and dragged herself along his orgasm-sensitive body, not caring whether sweat or semen coated her silk peignoir. For a moment, she listened to his harsh breaths, then she captured his mouth with hers, feeling his startlement as she pushed some of his own reproductive fluid between them, but he relaxed, resting his head in her cupped hand, and he took everything she gave him, hungry to experience it all, happy to please her.

She could feel her peaked nipples brushing against his chest through the clinging silk with each breath. She wanted to spread her confined thighs and push against him, watching his beautiful Earl Grey eyes as they widened and narrowed at her movements. But she waited. She had all night, all night to make him feel as marvelous as she did right now, riding the high of his *petite mort* and her ability to coax it from him.

More himself now, he tugged at his wrists slightly, moving them to get her attention. "You are the most amazing woman I have ever met. Shall we undo these now and let me show you how much I esteem you?"

Wickedly, she grinned at him. If he thought the freedom of bondage was only a short respite from the world, he was very wrong. Still, his desire to rebuff her gift-bindings rankled. "I think I like you this way," she said, sitting up to straddle his waist once again and making no move to untie him from her headboard. "In fact, I plan to keep you here for hours."

A slight softening around his eyes—*a release of anxiety perhaps?*—let her know that had been the right choice. Not giving him a chance to regroup, she whipped off her nightdress, dropping it beside the bed in a green puddle.

"You have no choices." She slid upward and dangled a bared breast over his mouth which he obediently, enthusiastically, surged forward to suck. She felt the wet heat all the way to her lungs, stuttering her breathing. "You have no escape."

He moaned around her nipple at this exotic promise, and she could barely handle this teasing she orchestrated. Her quim was no doubt full of lubrication by this point, warm and tingling over his chest, and the few points of contact couldn't possibly be enough to bring her to conclusion, only to more and more frustration. But she wasn't ready yet for this to be over. God, she never wanted it to be over.

His sucking pulls on her breast got stronger, and she pulled out only to be rewarded by a displeased whine. Well, if he wanted more, he'd get more. She inched up the bed to put a knee just above each shoulder.

Tenderly, she stroked his face, giving him a chance to protest, even though that seemed unlikely at this point. Still, fun and games were one thing; forcing someone was something else. She needn't have worried. For a moment, he nuzzled into her stroking hand; then he moved away to kiss the thigh next to his head.

And then she was worlds away as his tongue swept up and down her reddened lips before swirling in maddening circles around her itching nub. It was too much, and she wanted to run away from his magnificent mouth that made her all untwisted. But it wasn't enough, and she wanted to feel more of him, to rub against him and be so caught up in him that she was he and he was her.

Ah! She lost track of desires and intentions when he nibbled on her. No, this wouldn't do. She had every right to bring him to another climax, and she wanted to come off around him.

This time when she pulled away, he barely had the chance for the displeased whining before she lined herself up and sunk down onto his member, hard again though she knew it would be some time before he could erupt. Not wanting to leave his mouth empty, she leaned forward and possessed his mouth with hers. He gave himself over easily to her passion, opening and gentling her need with his slow movements. Yes, slow. She could do slow.

For all her greedy appetites, she stilled and righted herself, holding him deeply within her body and simply feeling. Feeling every involuntary shift of his pelvis inside of her most intimate place. Feeling every breath he took in her rise and fall relative to the room. Feeling every willing secession of power in his wide, glassy eyes and self-enforced stillness.

She watched him for uncounted moments, wanting to be sure of his enjoyment. And then his eyes slipped closed, and his head twisted on the pillow, and she knew he was ready for more. Cara rolled her hips in a small motion, delighting in the dual push and pull against her inner walls and outer lips.

Again. Again. Not speeding up, nor slowing down. The movements came easier and easier, testament to her enjoyment, but her whole attention focused on her partner: on his face, his chest, his helpless mewls of desire. She curved her back to lip his nipples, and he cried out beneath her.

Restlessly, his pelvis shifted beneath her, but only slightly, as her weight and her legs locked him in place. Mindless, he scrabbled at the headboard, at his ties, and now she felt secure in her ability to let go and let passion run its course and still bring him to the ultimate peak.

They pushed against each other on the bed, a gasping, desperate, messy arrangement. With every strong roll of her hips, she tightened her muscles around him and she rubbed her pearl on his stomach. She arched her back and dug her toes into the duvet, getting as much traction as possible to bring them together more tightly. Her fingers came up to her breasts, plucking at nipples and drawing a tingling, sharp pleasure from chest to groin and pooling in that place inside where she held him prisoner.

Push, pull. Rub, roll. She arched even more strongly, clamping down on him as her fingers clamped down on her reddened, pinched nipples. Her whole body strained to attain that ultimate goal until silently, she slumped down, her only tell a quiet groan.

He continued pumping into her, smaller motions now as he tried to respect her space. But she felt him across her oversensitive skin, and her throbbing internal muscles flexed and shuddered against him.

Dragging herself up, she knew she had to finish him. He shivered at the loss of warmth when her body uncoupled, but made no complaint. Again, she eased herself between his legs to take hold of his member. It glistened with her fluids, her mark of possession. A few short strokes from her hand, and he came apart again, semen more clear than white for this second bursting.

She drew alongside him, lining up flush with his side to kiss him one more time. She felt oddly empty, untouched in her soul for all that her body had come to the ultimate fulfillment. Maybe a brief cuddle would bring her back into the present, give her that sense of *togetherness* she sought. Intending to loose him and perhaps curl under the covers for a few hours, she reached for the ties at his wrists.

Stanley shook his head. "Not yet." His voice was small, pleading. "Please, just a little longer."

She ran her fingers down from the ties, over his forearms, and down to his waist. Tucking herself against his side, she settled in for a short nap, ready to release him whenever he was ready.

Chapter Five – David

David McAlpine had followed the uppity cove over all Londontown for a week now. He couldn't say as he saw the reason for that slippery errand, but Geoffrey Black, that right man who'd bought the porter and listened to his St. Crossian woes, told him to watch and wait. Then they'd come to that varmint together, and *together* they'd force the cardsharp's hand, where McAlpine couldn't do so alone.

He didn't know how they'd use the information he'd gathered. It was entirely times, events, and what the townhouse bought in vittles.

Then again, he still hadn't sussed Mr. Black's interest in St. Cross. He'd asked once, and Mr. Black had explained about St. Cross's being part of the Caller Club. One enemy of his also held a membership, a Marquis of Greenhope—something about a married woman and her pocketbook. Through St. Cross, Mr. Black hoped to gain access to the marquis, but McAlpine didn't know how that might work out.

McAlpine didn't know a lot of things. He'd been

about to head home to the farm, cold and hungry, leaving St. Cross to his ill-won gains. But Geoffrey Black had given him this one final chance to repair his meager fortunes, and McAlpine meant to take advantage.

He entered the warm public house, fire still stoked and air moist from drinks and humanity, even at this late hour. The blue-aproned publican recognized him on sight and pulled a dark pint, one that McAlpine didn't have to pay for. Ah, the perks of working with the mysterious Mr. Black. Unlimited credit at this house made up for all the to-ing and fro-ing in his enemy's wake.

As if summoned by McAlpine's thoughts of his largesse, Mr. Black joined him at the bar. He ordered a paler pint and made a show of toasting their glasses. "Tonight's the night. We're going to win back your necessity from Miss St. Cross."

He hadn't been able to teach his benefactor to say *Mister* St. Cross, even though all of London called the nip by that title. "But he's done nothing other than play cards, the swindler. What's the news?"

"Exactly. After her duel with my marquis, no ills have befallen her. Thus, she must be in full membership with Callers, ay? My part, then, is taken into account. Your part has been ready since the second day we met."

It has? This intelligence came for the first time to McAlpine. "Ay?" Now the smarter man had him saying it.

Mr. Black grinned and leaned in conspiratorially. "After all, you only need to get her out of the house and marry her."

Marry St. Cross? He'd come to London to get his money back, to take it out of her house—*damn, he'd called the man 'her'*—all unknown, a vengeful retribution with no interpersonal element nor side effects. "I'm not for him!" he protested, careful of his pronouns.

Mr. Black pounded him on the back and laughed like he'd told a joke. "You'll be saving all the country, ay? You get your money and all her dowry collection while making certain she never defrauds another man again. Make her a woman, and she'll be no trouble at all."

McAlpine had seen his mother and sisters wrap their husbands up in petticoats, and thought St. Cross could do it to him just as easily. Then again, those lasses made *real* women, not poker players and adventurers. Maybe making her live in his style would give him the advantage of her.

Yes, this sounded reasonable. He would marry St. Cross, take control of her amassed fortune, bring her back to his farm in the country, and live in a more comfortable manner: with a wife who could cook, clean, and look after him. He'd always envied his sisters' husbands for their well-kept homes and easy dinners after a day in the fields.

He tossed back his pint and scraped back from the bar. "Let's go get me a wife."

Mr. Black stood and slung a cape over his shoulders, his pint undrained. "I have a small fiacre waiting out front, ay."

Indeed he did. McAlpine leapt into the covered box while Black took the reins of the two-horse team, the extra horse for speed. To Shaftesbury Square they went.

* * *

Mr. Black *whoa*ed the horses in front of St. Cross's residence direct. No dilly-dallying about. No riding the street to make certain of empty doorways where no one lingered. No stopping two or three houses down in order to deter suspicion when the man, lady, went missing.

The pair of them tied the horses, then walked right up to the front door, entitled as you please. McAlpine supposed the townhouse *almost* belonged to him since his betrothed called it home, but no one else knew that. Something about Mr. Black, his surety, kept anyone from catching them out. Speaking of, where was the fearsome manservant who'd run McAlpine off the week before?

"She's given her help the night off, ay," Mr. Black said after he'd convinced the locked front door to open and bowed McAlpine into the foyer. "Let's 'em rest every week on this one night."

That made sense, McAlpine supposed. He expected he'd use that night off for procreational purposes once St. Cross became his comfortable importance.

This time of evening, if anyone sat easy at home, they did so in the rooms upstairs. His puddings roiled with nerves, but not a single step creaked nor floorboard roared. Slow as church work, they made their way up until they stood on the landing deck and surveyed the layout.

Mr. Black pointed down one hallway. "You'll go right, ay? I'll take the left, and we'll meet back here with the hoyden."

McAlpine sniffed. Why, if this weren't Mr. Black, he'd beat the man for those words. "That's my intended you're discussing!" he protested as quietly as he could. "I'll thank you to keep a civil tongue." His mama had said the same thing to him many a time.

The other man bent a hind leg in mocking apology, and McAlpine counted that sense enough.

Kemp's shoes, what providence! A door creaked open, and out stepped his lady, all city-soft and wrapped in green silk. On spying Mr. Black, she sucked in a loud breath, preparing to speak, but McAlpine came up behind her and knocked her on the head, catching her afore she fell to her marrowbones. Women fell to a farmer's blow just like any other animal would; the amount of force laid the trick in all renderings.

With great care, he transferred the lady into Mr. Black's arms, being sure to rearrange her robes into perfect folds, for only a slamkin would go outside in such state as she'd fallen. "We meet again at the Toll House in Coldstream," McAlpine said, patting his wife-to-be's clasped hands. "I've a mind to look through the house for my screen."

"Don't be a natural fool." Why would Mr. Black whisper if the house sat empty tonight? "The scratch falls to you when you speak your vows in Scotland."

Sense and true. But McAlpine couldn't just leave without taking something. Besides, if everything near belonged to him already, what did it matter to Mr. Black if he took his own with him? "All the same." Like oxen and donkeys, McAlpines stood their own.

"I'll leave a horse for you." Smart of Mr. Black to realize McAlpine didn't plan to follow blindly. "You'll catch us up on the road, ay? We make Coldstream in three days of hard travel." Three days, and he'd have more money than a man could easily count and a wither-go-ye of his own.

But when he opened the door to the room St. Cross had just left, his eyes met with a more unexpected piece of ill luck than imagined.

Her bedroom glowed with soft candle and electric lights. The serviceable wooden furniture gleamed its polish along thick lines. And a poor, kidnapped man lay naked in the center of the bed. Didn't she know kidnapping was illegal? Who could the unfortunate bloke be, and what did St. Cross have against him? For now, McAlpine could only apologize to the fellow.

McAlpine hurried to the gorger's side, hands immediately going to the green ties at his wrists. St. Cross really did have a penchant for green, didn't she? She'd like summers in the country then, the green hills and plant dyes.

"Whatever's going on, man?" demanded the unclothed victim. He flexed his freed fingers and watched McAlpine's motions with angry eyes, not that anyone could blame the gentle for his anger.

"Don't know how long you've been prisoner here, mister, but the chit's gone now, and she's never bothering you again." McAlpine loosed the remaining bonds and stood to hunt for the gentleman's clothes. "Don't you worry. My man and I are taking her out to Coldstream, and no wife of mine jails London men."

The man took a shaky step. He must've been here a long time. "St. Cross is your wife?"

"She will be by the end of the week." McAlpine passed over the clothes he'd found, then started rooting through drawers for his objective. The promissory notes on top all stood for too much money. He'd never get a moneylender to accept one, and the issuers would ask too many questions about St. Cross. "And then you'll be perfectly safe."

"Yes, yes. Thank you." The man sounded distracted, but McAlpine expected that from a man recently freed with the promise of security from his captor. "Coldstream by the end of the week, you say?"

"It'll take that long to ride there." Speaking of riding to Scotland, McAlpine grabbed some pretty baubles from the surface of his lady's vanity, then stuffed some finery into a valise in her closet. No need for the woman to go about in scraps when she had all this at home. "All the best, sir. And please don't mention this to anyone."

"No, no, of course not." The man's voice already sounded stronger. "I wouldn't want anyone to know I'd been tied up at that harridan's mercy."

McAlpine let the insult slide. The gorger *had* just been tied up and captured for whatever perfidious scheme his lady ran. With a bow, he left the man to his own devices.

McAlpine would catch up to Mr. Black and St. Cross on the road. No doubt, she'd be thrilled to see him and the goodies he brought along, even though he intended to vamp some pretties for ready money. Once she'd settled in to life with him at his farm cottage, she wouldn't need such meaningless things.

Chapter Six – Stanley

For silent moments after the strange man left, Stanley stood still, watching his clothes and the walls, but not truly seeing anything. *They've captured Cara!*

She'd been long gone by the time Stanley had pretended disinterest to the stranger in the bedroom, but now the fact collided with his mindsprings at full spin. In his rush to don trousers and shirt, he nearly stumbled over himself. The bare minimum would have to be enough. He had no time to waste.

Quickly, now, he had to run after them. The man had declared his destination as Coldstream, had sworn himself *to marry St. Cross.* Not while Stanley lived. He would not let his friend be so poorly used.

Shirt unbuttoned, shoeless, he threw open the door to the hallway. "Children!" he called for Cara's servants. They deserved to know their mistress's fate and might be trusted to lend him their fastest horse. Rush wild, he'd mount it after the miscreants and bring them to justice, thereby saving his... whatever Cara was.

The girl and boy he'd seen before crowded into the hall with him, it not being designed for so many personages, illustrious or otherwise. He tried to stride between them, he being far larger and more muscled than they, but they kept him pinned and unable to reach the stairwell.

He didn't have time for this! He needed to press his pursuit of the odd kidnapper and could fill the servants in as he headed for the door. Cara was all alone and helpless amongst men who intended to destroy her life. The children needed to move.

Somehow the girl maneuvered behind him, still keeping him in place. "Where's our lady gone?"

Stanley whirled to keep his focus on her, almost dizzying himself with the speed. Why didn't these youngsters stay out of his way? He simply needed them to deliver a fast horse so he could solve all their problems. "At least two men took her. One told me they headed for Coldstream to make her his wife." He growled the last word. Cara chose her own path just as society chose Stanley's, but neither of them should be thwarted by petty thieves.

"I'll call you a carriage," said the boy with a firm nod, looking beyond the marquis to his compatriot. "Meanwhile, I'll fetch the Guard."

The girl ducked into a doorway for a frustrating few moments wherein the boy refused to answer Stanley's requests for passage or a fast horse. She soon emerged, however, to take hold of Stanley's arm in a firm, leather-gloved grip. "I'll take his lordship with me to go after milady."

Why, she was just a young girl! But a quick look at his enforced companion showed her well-outfitted for the job. Unlike the house dress she'd worn in service, now she sported a leather suit from head to toe, all in dark brown that matched her tightly plaited hair. At her hips, two pistols waited to fire, and Stanley believed he could make out the outlines of knife handles in her sleeves, which explained the gloves, really.

"Well?" said the walking armory. "What're you waiting for? Nathan's carriage is probably here already."

How dare she accuse him of languishing when the two conspirators had kept him trapped? Why, he'd have left already if the boy weren't still blocking his path.

Only, the boy had gone while Stanley had paused to admire the bristling weaponry on his self-appointed companion. Resigned to being outwitted by the wily youths of London's seedy underbelly, uplifted by a lady to whom they must be deeply beholden and enamored, Stanley let himself be tugged down the stairs to a waiting curricle. He didn't even complain of the cold, coal-tainted wind in his face.

He did, however, complain about the direction they took. Coldstream was to the north, of course, in Scotland where the marriage laws had a certain laxity about them. But the girl had directed their conveyance to the east. Yes, their destination lay to the northeast, but something smacked of oddness and unnecessarily out-of-the-way diversions. "Whyever are we heading this way?"

She didn't turn to look at him, hunched forward and squinting into the distance. "We need help," she said. "Viscount Althorp has horses."

While Althorp's horses would indeed be welcome, Stanley preferred not to arrive at the man's residence in the dead of night with only a mutual friend's servant girl for company. He had no better ideas, though, and the stop would necessarily be mercifully short. Afterwards, well, he and Althorp had little in common besides St. Cross. Hopefully, that acquaintance would keep his mouth quiet even as their joint excursions faded.

The horse's hooves clattered to a halt on a stone bridge, and the girl leapt from the carriage. She waved her arms in large windmills, jumping up and down and looking quite silly. More sedately, Stanley alighted from the curricle, passing the driver a small coin for his service.

"Hey, up there!" the girl shouted to whomever stood watch that night on Tower Bridge.

By Heaven! She didn't mean to enter the Tower? Though, come to think of it, he'd never visited with Althorp, whom he'd assumed lived in his family's London townhouse. A military man, he very well could be staying with friends at the regiment who housed here. Wasn't Althorp Navy, though?

The guards apparently recognized the girl, since they lifted gate after gate to allow her through. As soon as the last iron and wood parted, she pelted down slick cobbles and over grass to the innermost ward. Fit though he was, Stanley barely caught up to her at the door to the Commander's Residence, where she pounded the wooden planks as though she might burst through them.

A young sergeant in regimental red opened the door at her summons. "Miss Mindy! What are you doing here at this time of night?"

"No time, Monty," she panted out, slowing to speak with him while still making her way towards another part of the residence at speed. The girl must have accompanied her mistress on calls to Althorp many a time. "Let the viscount know I'm in the drawing room?"

Stanley gave the poor man an apologetic glance, but the sergeant just grinned while bowing to him. Stanley had to wonder if the man were a little bit in love with the girl. Something about her decisive and commanding nature would surely appeal to a man used to military life. After all, it had appealed to *him.*

"Lord Greenhope!" the girl called from somewhere ahead.

He followed the sound of her voice to a large waiting room. He supposed this made up a military commander's drawing room, plenty of space for entertaining officers and impressing the lower ranks. Repurposed from its old days as a royal castle, it still held the gravitas of its former glory, and certainly had enough space for military billeting.

Then they waited.

With every step the girl took, pacing the carpets and glancing pointedly at a case-less clock, Stanley's ire grew. She had no right to force him from his purpose, to derail him from the critical job of finding and rescuing Cara. Why, at this very moment, that lady could be undergoing horrid tortures and outrages, and when he finally found her, she'd ask him, *Why didn't you save me, Stanley?*

They didn't need Althorp. They only needed his horses, which the girl could clearly appropriate on her own merit without needing to stand around in this over-heated drawing room in the middle of a royal garrison. Stanley vibrated with the urge to move. He could simply put one foot in front of the other, then go find that sergeant.

But he didn't. He stood perfectly still, showing good breeding and posture while the girl paced and bounced and showed all manner of the impatience Stanley fought so hard to hide.

He had to admit, according to the clock they hadn't waited all that long before Althorp arrived. Only a minute or two in the drawing room, and the viscount entered through an oversized wooden doorway that had doubtless been left open due to its sheer, bulky weight. Bright-eyed and perfectly groomed even at this outlandish hour, Althorp paused near the door to turn a knob on the wall. Stanley heard a few clicks before a beautiful waltz melody started. He looked around to discover the source of this supposedly soothing irritant.

"Snuck out on your own tonight, little Miss Mindy?" Althorp greeted his guests less politely than Stanley would have expected, but perhaps the man hadn't seen him yet.

"My lady's been kidnapped," Mindy said. No preamble and no histrionics. "We think she's *en route* to Scotland."

"We?" Althorp looked past the girl in the firelight, hunting for her companion. When he saw Stanley, his eyebrows arched up in that peculiar way, undoubtedly interpolating his presence. "My apologies, Lord Greenhope. I wasn't expecting you."

But he expected guests from St. Cross's household in the middle of the night? "No offense taken, Lord Althorp. I wish I could have visited under less dire circumstances."

"Damn," said Althorp, though Stanley didn't think he took offense at the small talk. "This has something to do with those men who've been following her about, doesn't it?"

This was the first Stanley had heard of anyone's stalking St. Cross, himself excepted. "The first thief took her from the house," Stanley summarized, "and the second explained his plan to marry her at Coldstream. For her money, most likely, since he also rooted through her belongings on his way out."

None of the three mentioned aloud by what occasion Stanley should be present for the midnight happenings, nor for talks with the kidnappers.

Now that Althorp had been filled in, the girl spoke up. "I think we should ride out, pick her up, and shoot anyone who gets in our way." The no-nonsense delivery belied the eager gleam of candlelight on her many pearl stocks.

"I shall ask my host for his fastest, most tireless horses," said Althorp, much to Stanley's pleasure. *Here* was the reason the girl had come after a man who resided at a royal garrison.

Against all expectations, however, Althorp did not immediately go to find this host, but quickly crossed to a writing desk and opened the mahogany top. He rifled through a drawer and slammed a few sheets of paper onto the bared surface. Then he reached into a cubby full of cylindrical objects in the back, turned it perpendicular to the sheaves, and cranked a small handle on the side. Stanley saw the ink mixing itself inside the head of what he now recognized as a mechanical pen.

"Cara is imperiled, and you're doing your *corre-spondence*?" Stanley heard his voice shriek up at the end, but couldn't bring himself to apologize.

"Cara, is it?" Althorp didn't look up from the desk or remove his pen from the paper till he signed one with a flourish, folded and addressed it, and moved onto the next.

Devil take the man. Whatever Stanley called her, the woman needed their help. The rogues probably had her halfway to Scotland, drugged and tied, still in the silky shift she'd worn during their exertions. Yet, instead of rushing to her aid, he worked on his social niceties within the *ton*.

Another paper folded and addressed, Althorp pulled a bell cord. "Get ahold of yourself, Greenhope. We're no good to Crossy without a plan. If these men have been after her for at least a week, then she's not safe in London. What do you plan to do after the rescue, hmm?"

Stanley should have reminded Althorp that after-rescue plans didn't much matter if the woman had already been killed or married off before they reached her. Instead, he parried the man's earlier question of address. Let *him* cast stones. "Crossy, is it?"

"My pardon. I'd believed you to be inside St. Cross's circle of close friends, close enough to use the name."

A smirk crossed the man's face, and Stanley realized that perhaps he'd been a bit demanding and, dare he say, annoying for someone in his position. Who was he to call Althorp out on an innocent bit of nicknaming? Not when he'd just called their connection *Cara*, a right Althorp possibly didn't have.

However, he'd already committed to the course of *affronted gentleman* and could not choose to turn back now. "I've never heard anyone call St. Cross any such thing." He hoped he'd correctly intimated what society might think.

A yeoman appeared in the doorway. "Sir?"

Althorp stood to give the man the addressed letters. After the yeoman left, Althorp took measured steps towards Stanley, the deliberation of someone holding in their anger, but only just.

"Listen here, Greenhope. You and I both know what you were up to this evening, though you'd just called St. Cross out for fictitious relations with your wife. I shall ignore the situation out of love for St. Cross. Because whatever personal rapport you have, I have a kinship with him all my own.

"You may not have noticed, Greenhope, that I have no place in London other than as St. Cross's friend. Three months ago, I resigned my Navy commission when both my father and my elder brother took ill, but I can't tend to them as I should since someone must survive to hold the Duke's title. So I wait, lamenting my commission's expiry, and as a Navy man, I know my work and how to be useful, none of this faffing about like a lickspigot at the tables of society.

"Nowadays, St. Cross is my closest companion. I have just as much at stake in this as you do. Probably more. So, yes, I'd like to be in your place. Yes, I'd like to call him *Cara*. But his safety and well-being mean more to me than a change in our relationship. So when I send out letters to secure St. Cross's future, don't talk to me of innuendo and dominance games."

Stanley had had no idea. No one at the club talked with Althorp much, and Stanley had only met him through St. Cross. He'd known on some level that the man was related to the Duke of Oxford, but it hadn't seemed relevant. That rather proved Althorp's point. Even at the Caller, he retained an air of aloof nonentity.

"I didn't realize you were so close to the royal family." It wasn't an apology, but it would do. Said in such a calm way, gently ignoring the emotional outburst of moments before, Althorp couldn't help but respond.

"Now you do. It's why I get to live in the Tower, even though I'm not in any of the billeted military regiments and never was."

Althorp had the right to continue his snappishness. Stanley could admit now that he'd ill-treated his fellow.

A higher-pitched voice, full of a teenager's eye-rolling frustration: "Milords!" The two gentlemen broke off their conversation to acknowledge the girl. "If you're done snapping and barking, the stables have sent our mounts around the front and added some flintlock rifles. Make haste!"

CHAPTER SEVEN - CARA

For two days, Cara suffered the indignities and unexpected discomforts of a kidnapping victim. While she might have expected the restraints, she'd certainly never imagined herself in such inappropriate garments when being spirited away. She'd begun their trip in her peignoir, then been offered a few bizarre choices McAlpine had acquired from her townhouse.

When they'd first changed horses, they'd acquired and bundled her into an itchy woolen dress—the meager sort she'd worn in childhood, certainly not the thing Mr. St. Cross might condescend to wear. Even with its greater coverage, the dress couldn't shield her from the blowing November winds rushing through the open carriage.

From the way the men spoke amongst themselves, Cara believed the two lawbreakers had long planned this escapade together, though the two vile species-defilers acted as differently as bridge players and patience players.

The sun shimmered in the darkening sky when Black snapped the reins to speed the horses yet faster. "How now, missy. Don't you want to discuss happier times?

Perhaps tell me about your friends at the Caller Club. Perhaps you met the Marquis of Greenhope, ay?"

Black doubtless thought his questions subtle, but he had revealed a passion for all things Greenhope during the first day of their trip, and it tainted his otherwise smooth demeanor. As yet, he never mentioned her illicit affair, so Cara didn't believe he knew anything about it.

"He's not much of a poker player." She didn't ask for a cloak. She wouldn't give either abuser any leverage.

"You're in a terrible pucker now, horrid beast." McAlpine tried to loom over her whilst sitting beside her in the coach and helpfully pushing her windblown hair behind her ears. "You should tell Mr. Black anything he needs to know. Besides, I'll order you to tell him anyway once we're married."

She barely held in her laughter. The man had strange thoughts about the nature of spousal power, especially over a woman who'd been so independent as to live like a man. A more successful man than he, by the looks of things.

Cara thought she understood what Black wanted from her, information about his target—Lord Greenhope—from a person he viewed as the weakest gasket at the Caller Club. But McAlpine held an entirely different hand. "Whyever should you wish to marry me, sir?" She'd long learned to disarm men by calling them by titles.

McAlpine took to petting her hair with a soothing calm. "Don't you worry. I'm not rocked in a stone kitchen. But you owe me money, *you scaly scab*." How quickly he switched from solicitous to angry, as if he couldn't separate his supposed enemy, Mr. St. Cross, from his delicate future wife.

"Would you care for a game of chess?" asked Black, apropos of nothing. The small fiacre held little room for a game box.

McAlpine sighed forcefully. "Oh, don't ask again. You know my prowess is that of a solo player."

This time Cara did let escape a tired giggle. They'd kept her up all night and day, and McAlpine's ability to admit his failings struck her with force. For a man who knew where his strengths rested, he involved himself with unlikely characters in unlikely plots.

Black gave out a disparaging grunt. "I didn't mean you, did I, ay? I meant the gambling queen. Maybe she'll deign to teach me her wily tricks and explain how she procured an invitation to the Caller Club."

"If you truly desire the game, sir," she said as meekly as possible, "you'll have to free my hands from their bonds." She contrived to shrink back against McAlpine, letting his bulk make her smaller in comparison. She could taste a cautious freedom.

Unfortunately, her action also prompted the country man to offer, "I'll move your pieces, my chuck. Let me help you."

Foiled!

"Would you set the board, McAlpine?" Black's hands stayed busy on the reins of the speedy horses, hastening to Mr. St. Cross's demise and Mrs. McAlpine's birthplace. "Have you ever met the marquis of Greenhope's wife, Miss St. Cross? A lovely lady to be sure."

Bastard. Did he think to make her jealous of her lover's attachments? She'd known full well that Greenhope had a lady. They'd dueled over her, after all. "I'm afraid I've never met her," she replied. To McAlpine, she pointed out, "The knight goes one square over. No, the other way."

McAlpine growled, but then politely thanked her. He appeared to be neither a passive player nor an aggressive one, and she found it hard to peg him. If she truly owed him money, shouldn't he come to her residence and show her the promissory note? If he wished to make a wifely home, wouldn't he better serve himself by finding a suitable woman?

Black's attention remained on the road, though his head wagged from side to side like a novice attempting to read his seatmates' cards. Could some soul have joined them on the road? "Lady Greenhope is a particular friend of mine." His voice gave no hint of apprehension, unlike his posture. "A venerable woman with an overbearing, dull husband, as all of his class describe, ay?"

Either Black hoped to catch her out in Stanley's passionate defense, or he wanted her sympathy for the adulteress. Her own circumstances made her a biased listener. Hoping to trip him into a revealing monologue, she simply echoed, "A particular friend?"

He started in his seat. "Gag her," he ordered.

McAlpine reached into his pocket for the wet ball of material they'd only removed from her mouth after passing Doncaster. "How'll she tell me where to put her pieces if I make the cull easy?"

Dull thuds added their noises to the road, out of time with the panting two-horse team. Someone *had* come upon them. She opened her mouth to cry, but McAlpine caught the motion and the meaning quickly enough, stuffing her with cloth till her scream came out a kitten's mew. Kicking a slipper-shod foot, she managed only to overturn the chessboard, not even to startle Black into swerving the fiacre.

A shot rang out, and the top of their carriage found itself in possession of a small hole. Doubtless, a warning gambit, but enough to brighten Cara's hopes. These unknowns intended to halt the coach. Maybe highwaymen with no personal interest in her. Maybe friends. Either way, she'd find a better position in their clutches than in these.

"Hyah!" Black goaded the team to greater speeds, sour sweat dripping from his ears. "Almost there. Almost."

Up ahead, she could see a stone bridge. At the other end, if she squinted, she could see lights in the windows of a single-story toll house. This, then, must be Cold-stream. She shivered. *Damned if I'm letting them take me without a fight, especially with salvation so close.*

She kicked again, causing a fiery pain in her barely protected toes as she attempted to dislodge Black from his seat or his purpose. This time, she caught his nearest arm, and the carriage twisted at the diagonal, now heading for the riverbank. He tried to pull them back on course, but at those speeds, his strength couldn't match two determined thoroughbreds.

The horses stumbled and screamed as they clattered over uneven rocks coated in coral-like fungus. Then the fiacre began to slow, mired in muddy muck. The wheels slammed into a particularly spiky rock and one broke, throwing McAlpine bodily from the carriage and tumbling Cara into his seat. Still, Black hauled the reins, not at all disturbed by his compatriot's disappearance.

Dark-brown horse legs flashed past her side of the cab, strong and loud, but not as loud as the next shot. Black's paler horses reared back with the close shock, splashing the interior of the fiacre with freezing river water and bringing their progress to a halt.

The dark horse stood in front of them, and Cara looked up into the grey sky to see a tiny figure bristling with firearms. The figure pointed at Black a gold pistol with a large circle, like an Irish sunburst, between the stock and the barrel. "You'll hand over the lady now," said the figure. "Or I'll rotate twenty-four projectiles through your brain."

Mindy! Bless her little heart.

Black laughed. "Go home, little girl. Find some other coach to rob." He thought her a knight of the road, but no matter. Mindy clearly had the upper hand.

With Black distracted, Cara threw herself from the fiacre, rolling on sharp stones. She inhaled water on a gasp. She couldn't drown so close to rescue and the shore! Thrashing and twisting, she attempted to turn over so she could float on her back in the River Tweed.

Sharp hooves clattered on rocks near her head, but she couldn't spare the worry that they'd bash her head open. A strong hand grasped the back of her heavy wool dress, made all the heavier by the soaking. She rose through the air till she laid face down across a saddle, unknown hands stripping the gag, then thumping her back and forcing the water from her lungs.

Friend or foe? Till she knew, Cara didn't intend to remain in this undignified position. If McAlpine had filched a horse to take her across the bridge and carry out his mission, she'd no obligation to make it easy for him. She threw her weight backwards, catching her savior-captor's groin with her shoulder. He grunted and curled forward, his hands leaving her back, and Cara slipped off the saddle to rest bare feet in the riverbed.

Free at last, Cara looked up to see Althorp grasping at the pommel, wearing a gaping grimace of pain. He'd come to save her, and this was how she repaid him. On her honor, she was the worst friend and companion a person could have. After all Althorp had done for her, the good times they'd shared, she betrayed him so cruelly when he stood in her defense? "Oh, Al. I'm so sorry. What can I do?" She looked up at him with pleading eyes, hoping he'd see the genuine remorse in them.

"Think nothing of it, Crossy," he said, barely loud enough that she could hear him over the ringing in her ears.

His mouth moved on something else, but she couldn't make it out over the sound of rifle-fire. They both whirled to see the Coldstream Regiment in their crimson coats jogging over the bridge. Althorp moved his horse to shield her and waved to the approaching force, signaling camaraderie and lack of aggression.

"Die, bitch!" Black's voice echoed across the river. He'd wrested Mindy from her seat and now posed over her sprawled form with the hunter's gun from the driver's box.

The newcomers were too far away, and Cara herself could not cross the distance in her sopping dress. She fisted her hands as though that might somehow get her close enough to change the inevitable.

Before he could cock the gun, Black fell to the side, bowled over by another figure, one broader and taller than Cara's other two rescuers. Mindy scrambled to her feet and unsheathed a knife, her firearms having all soaked in the river. But, though she darted around the grappling couple, she never dashed forward to slice at one.

Black's surprised exclamation rang across the battle-field. "Greenhope!"

Stanley? Of course Stanley. He'd been the only one at her townhouse who could have known she was missing. Mindy might have been first on the scene, but Stanley had to be the one who'd discovered her plight. Had he called for help from her bed? And why would a man with his own resources have gone to Al?

She wanted to ask, but Althorp too had been un-seated. His riderless horse stomped to join the others, leaving her vulnerable to the Coldstream riflemen and giving her a view of Althorp and McAlpine tussling on the muddy bank.

Unable to influence either fight with her hands bound, she used the one faculty at her disposal. "Help!" she cried out to the regimental men who had almost arrived on scene. "Help!"

The men in red may not have heard her, but the vile kidnappers certainly stood close enough. Their fighting changed, no longer an effort to subdue but to separate. McAlpine extricated himself from Al's deadly embrace first, then worked towards Black.

Now on the scene, two scarlet coats moved to restrain Althorp, already motionless in the grassy mud. A third unbound Cara's hands.

The moment she was freed, Cara ran forward to drop to her knees in the muck at Althorp's side, holding his head in her lap. "Don't do this to me, Al. Not after you came all this way." She carded her fingers through his near-black hair, loose now around his face.

The armed men stepped back politely. "This your man, miss?" one of them asked.

God, yes. She'd certainly claim Al if it meant his safety. Since she'd joined the Caller Club, he'd become her fastest friend, the one she turned to when she needed advice, the one she trusted with her wards, the one she shared her troubles with. He most definitely belonged to her.

She nodded for the regimental's benefit. "He came to save me." She threw in a few tears, to play the emotions of the armed man. Unsurprisingly, the water flowed easily. With so much upheaval, so much relief to see her dearest friends in her darkest moment, her tears were real.

Soon, Mindy and Stanley joined their party, and the latter watched with narrowed eyes as Althorp brought his hand up to hold hers still against his cheek.

A short, round man, thick with muscle, pushed through the ranks of soldiers. He wore a red coat of his own, but covered it in decorations. The men all quickly removed themselves from his path. "One of you is Viscount Althorp, I hope." His voice was gruff and his speech was short on manners, but his blunt approach soothed Cara's nerves. Here was a person in charge, and on their side.

"I'm Lord Greenhope," Stanley said, bowing. "The unfortunate man on the ground is Lord Althorp." Stanley stood proud and strong. He'd hared across all of England, fresh from her bed. She remembered the look of him, all tied up at her mercy, and contrasted that with his powerful command now. God, he was gorgeous and perfect, in bed and out of it.

"The General at the Tower sent word by semaphore," the short man told Althorp, for all that Stanley had spoken first and outranked the gentleman in her lap. "We'll extend our hospitality to all of your party."

Al levered himself up to stand in front of the short man. He gave a small bow, though it made him waver in an alarming manner, and then he gestured to the remaining combatants. "That would be all of us. I'm afraid the heinous perpetrators have made off."

The man shrugged, more Gallic than Gaelic. "I'll send someone after them. You may stay as long as you like."

Althorp said, "I thank you for your generosity. While I may take advantage for quite some time, these other three only have tonight. They fly for the American colonies in two days."

Cara couldn't have heard that right. "What?"

Althorp smiled benignly, a clear tell of nerves, and tucked her hand into the crook of his arm. She felt him leaning against her, however, and let him get away with the proprietary gesture. "I've arranged for you to leave England for a while, just until your attackers have been detained."

"What if I don't want to leave England?" Her life was here. Her friends.

"What if I told you about a high-stakes poker tournament in the colonial territory of Washoe?"

CHAPTER EIGHT – DAVID

They'd fled. Run away like startled cows, stampeding headlong into—what? Did Mr. Black yet have a destination in mind? McAlpine was starting to have second, third, and fourth thoughts about the past days' events. Spiriting away a British woman, following that with an ill-prepared marriage attempt, fighting with the bloody jacks, and now this stealing horses so as to rush to nowhere.

Well, back to London, clearly, since he recognized the ways at which they stood, without the horses now so they couldn't be pulled for the speak. Mr. Black led him on, mindlessly trekking towards some undisclosed location. They weaved up cobbled lanes, passed mum beggars starting to speak again at the end of their working hours. Up the lanes and over the bridges, till the streets widened and the houses that lined the ways stood well-equipt.

Mr. Black came to a halt in front of rough iron gates too old-fashioned to have the modern gear-and-pulley openers. In the dusky light, McAlpine saw perfectly trimmed grass sprawling yard after yard, for all that no goats milled in residence. Far in the distance, along a cobbled path, dormant rose bushes guarded the front doors and windows of a townhouse larger than any country manse McAlpine had entered. *This* was someone's city residence?

No one stopped Mr. Black when he opened the gate, McAlpine trailing after. The leader darted 'round to the servants' entrance, for all his other bold posturings, and gave greetings and horse busses to the cook they met in the hallway.

"Her ladyship awaits your pleasure in the study, sir," the old fly-by-night informed Mr. Black with a wink.

They reached the study, a room overflowing with opulence beyond McAlpine's greatest expectations. He'd believed St. Cross's townhome the height of elegance, furnished with worked wood and dark carpets. But he knew now that it was a mere imitation of this expansive room, open yet cozy and full of all sorts of knickknacks. Here, a player piano. There, a mechanized sun-clock. On the far side, a bell pull.

And in the middle of the room stood a woman of such aristocratic bearing as to put all her surroundings to shame. Her shimmering blonde hair shone like the dawn sun over the field, all tied up in impossible curls. The paleness of it provided a bright contrast to her royal blue gown, somehow both modest and alluring at once. She surveyed the interlopers to her domain with a queen's disdain.

Mr. Black approached the goddess as though she held no power over him. With the panache of a pantomime hero, he swept her into his arms and kissed her soundly on the mouth, far too long and passionately for a public display. Then he pulled back, smiled into her flushed face, and struck her hard across the cheek. "Where is your husband, woman?"

Now more than ever, McAlpine really didn't want to be here.

The lady fell back onto a well-placed fainting couch, her hand rising to her wounded phys. "Fuck you too," she said. Such ghastly words should never leave such a beautiful mouth. But her eyes narrowed, and her voice formed more vileness till McAlpine couldn't recall how lovely he'd thought her. "I've received notice of divorce proceedings. This will ruin me. You said you'd take care of it, you bastard."

"Maybe the plot would move easier, lover, if you didn't keep your own counsel, ay? He wasn't meant to suspect your infidelity." Mr. Black didn't pace nor twitch. He portrayed the scary stillness of a marionette villain.

"Is that what you think?" the lady shrieked. Her voice hit new strides. "Then maybe you should have taken better care with your leavings." She huffed and turned away from the pair of them, reclining back onto her couch to convey how unimportant they were.

McAlpine had no trouble being unimportant to either of them.

Mr. Black stalked forward, his measured strides giving no indication of his thoughts. Gently, he settled beside her, and McAlpine tried not to watch him rub gentling circles on her nearer shoulder. "Shhh," Mr. Black soothed. "I have a plan. This will all work out for the best."

The lady began to make positive noises, and McAlpine averted his gaze, making himself swivel-eyed. He focused on a painting above the crackling fireplace, then took a closer look at it. "Ah, I only offer blind excuses for interrupting, but do you know the cove in that painting?"

Both occupants of the room turned to him with ire scrawled on their countenances.

"Tis the master of the house," the blonde offered slowly, "the Marquis of Greenhope."

Oh, he was under the hatches now. Mr. Black would never believe McAlpine lived all this time a looby. "It's only that I freed an unfortunate man from St. Cross's clutches who bore a marked resemblance."

Mr. Black remained preternaturally still, and McAlpine wished he'd form a fist or throw something. Anything. "You met this man at Miss St. Cross's residence?"

Before McAlpine could clarify that he'd been trying to help and hadn't thought the incident worth mentioning, the marchioness rounded on her sweetheart. "My husband has been seen with some other woman, and you didn't think we could blackmail him for the money?"

Attention again diverted from McAlpine, Mr. Black once more attempted to gentle his lover. "St. Cross hasn't acted the woman in public, and this news of infidelity comes late. Regardless, you know proof of his horn work means little before the Crown."

But the lady would not be clerked. "It would be enough to stay divorce proceedings!"

Mr. Black tilted his head in thought, then asked McAlpine, "What did you mean 'freed him'?"

"In her bedchamber, I hunted for blunt and found only vowel notes, those vile IOUs. In my search, I also found that man spread-eagled to the halberts in order to be whipped." McAlpine shivered at the thought. "How did such a small woman overpower him? We're not the only ones to underestimate the blackguard."

Mr. Black exploded from the longue. "You fool! You freed him not from torture but from a proud bitch."

McAlpine sucked in a breath. St. Cross played such games in her screwing? Better he'd escaped her marital clutches after all.

The lady stood behind Mr. Black and wrapped herself around him. "Wondrous news! We need only to make the marquis less of a man in society's eyes, and then I'll inherit all he has."

Mr. Black's hands came up to stroke her arms. "And what of me, my dear?"

She laid her head between his shoulder blades, the smile on her face a contrast to the darkening on Mr. Black's. "You'll always be welcome where I am."

Mr. Black reached into his waistband, then spun a fast figure. With a puncturing thrust, he slashed a hole in the lady's stomach and up through her rib cage. She fell to the floor in a puddle of blood and recriminations. Her dress darkened to a purple where the fibers soaked in the color.

Now Mr. Black paced, hands coated in her life flow. "Welcome? Welcome! Do you think I worked so hard to become your confidante, to plan your husband's downfall, only to be *welcome* in your bed? I wanted money and power, your position and influence." He towered over her cooling form, stashing his anger once more, as if gaining equilibrium removed him from God's black book. "You are useless to me now."

McAlpine tried to blend in with the background, like a slinking fox heading for the henhouse. But, like the fox, his natural predator found him out. McAlpine tried to halt disaster while it still resembled a minor scrape. "Looks like it's just the two of us."

Mr. Black stooped to pluck his knife from the former marchioness. "I can't have you speaking to the Bow Street Runners about tonight's doings. You understand, ay?"

McAlpine shook his head enthusiastically. "All this hoofing's been hard on my family and my livelihood. I'll just head back to my farm now, and never bother you or those justices of the Russian Coffee-house."

"It's not the farm you'll be visiting." Mr. Black leapt towards him.

McAlpine fell to the side, barely dodging the sharp blade that would chive him and mingle his blood with the superior kind. There! Next to the fireplace. Desperate, he scrambled on all fours for the only weapon he could see.

With a meaty *thunk*, like a larger knife into a cow's carcass, Mr. Black's knife found a home in McAlpine's back. McAlpine could feel the way it sliced and peeled with each breath and movement, but he still lived and still had a purpose. Unsteadily, he gained the fireplace and its poker. McAlpine pushed himself into a kneeling position, poker in hand like a javelin. Was it really worth spending his last breath on the man?

Mr. Black didn't have that hang-gallows look. He never had. "You won't get to marry St. Cross," he said, "but you'll take the blame for Lady Greenhope's demise. Not that it'll bother you much when you're dead, ay?"

"I'm no squirish squeeze wax to become your security!" McAlpine loosed the poker, saw it hit the center of Mr. Black's chest, and collapsed to the plush carpets. Death approached.

CHAPTER NINE - CARA

Two days penned up in the Coldstream's guest quarters took its toll. Cara would have left the whole place behind, but that only brought further complications—such as deciding where to go.

Mindy, at least, let her alone to think, making scarce by going off with the Guardsmen to practice riflery and fencing. Stanley and Al, though, preferred to terrorize each other and to team up on her whenever they took a moment away from infighting.

The marquis hovered, acting solicitous and guilty by turns, snapping at the recovering viscount on a second's notice for daring to breathe. Al, on the other hand, pressed and pressed Cara to leave. But not for her townhouse in London. Oh, no.

"I've got you a berth for four, Crossy. Take yourself and your staff over to the American colonies. You know they breed the Earth's canniest poker players."

While the gaming and the safety sounded lovely, Cara had no mind to be run out of town by some small-time kidnappers, to leave behind everything she'd gone to

London to find. She'd *worked* her way into the Caller Club. She couldn't just take Althorp's charity.

Stanley, of course, agreed on only one thing: protecting the *helpless lady.* "Indeed, my dear"—he seemed to feel it easier to treat her as a woman—"the idea has merit. Perhaps you would do me a great service and stake out a spot for my trading company in the Spanish west of that continent."

At least they're trying to bribe me instead of hustle me away willy-nilly. "I'm perfectly safe in London," she informed them both. "I shan't be treading new ground, especially in a country with no established gaming venues."

"You could start one!" Stanley nodded his head with the enthusiasm of a hopeful puppy. She half expected his tongue to loll out. "Your outpost for me could also be a branch of the Club. The locals would adore it, and any Englishmen coming through would appreciate the breath of civilization." He pressed hard, as though he could sense her thrill at the idea of owning her own establishment and exploring a new world. "Please. I am looking to expand in the colonies."

"Quite right, old chap." Al ignored Stanley's glare at the assumed familiarity. "Any man of the Caller would hate to be stuck outside the civilized parlors. You could rig that issue right."

Cara appreciated their concern, but her life was her own, and she finally had it organized to her own specifications. Though, opening a gambling house *did* have a certain appeal. "What makes you think *this* man of the Caller wants to be sent down from the *monde?*"

Al laughed and gestured to indicate all of her. "Tell me you're not the most adventurous member of our little Club. If any of us should go out to spread and multiply, it's bound to be you."

To that phraseology, Stanley apparently took exception. "Multiplying is not for gentle ladies."

Cara bristled. "*Mister* St. Cross is not a lady. *Particularly* not where the Club is concerned."

Both men ignored her. Althorp spoke only to Stanley. "I meant in terms of gathering like-minded novices."

"Still." Stanley wouldn't let the argument go. "Plenty of our members plan to involve their children, and their children's children. We shall easily multiply in the traditional manner."

If the Club lasted that long. To be fair, some salons and groups had hundreds of years' longevity, but most formed and collapsed in a comparative instant.

"At this rate," she broke in, aggravated at their lack to attention, "I shan't take either of you with me on that fourth ticket."

Stanley perked up, distracted from his bad temper. "So you'll go, then?"

She'd not said *that.*

Al waved away the threat. "I never expected to go. My adventuring days are over, regardless of my family's newly recovered health."

Cara sighed. To Stanley, she clarified, "I didn't say that." For Al, "And a pleasure cruise to the colonies is hardly devastating adventure." Corrections complete, she said, "I'm simply pointing out that you boys need to stow your animosity and focus on your mutual goals."

The both stiffened at the designation *boy.* Good. Let them. After the way they'd relegated her to incapable object, she could do the same.

Before either gentleman could express his ire and umbrage, the local commander entered. "I hate to intrude," he said—and Cara would have too, if she'd been him—"but I have good and bad news from Bow Street." Though the general appeared to address the room at large and ought to have directed his speech to Stanley, for rank, or Al, for connections, he chose instead to favor Cara with a pleading look.

"Do start with the good news first, General," she said. "We could all use some cheering."

He graced her with a small bow. "Your attackers have been found dead, madam. Murdered each other just the other night."

Al moved faster than the doctor said he ought, taking Cara in his arms and spinning her around in impromptu dance. Overcome with goodwill, he attempted to so engage Stanley as well, but the marquis suffered only a handshake.

Stanley extended that same stilted, over-formal gesture to her as well after completing it with Althorp. "Now your life is your own again."

Hadn't he been listening at all these last two days? "My life has always been my own, Greenhope, but it's nice of you to notice." She allowed herself the sharkish smile of a player holding a royal flush at a table of hustlers. "Or perhaps your words hold deeper meaning. Should I ruminate more deeply on your earlier urgings? Your suggestion of a gambling-waypoint in the territories may hold merit after all."

Stanley, the scheme's staunchest supporter only moments prior, hastened to gather back his discarded words. "You can't possibly want to undertake such an expedition!"

"I could have sworn you'd only just finished telling me what a capital idea and astounding adventure the whole plan was. My Nathan clearly has a head for the hotel business, and I've worked gaming tables before. Yes, it sounds marvelous... although a tad lonely."

Stanley latched onto that breadcrumb like a cribbage player who knew he shouldn't play a paired five but couldn't help himself. "Too true. The colonial territories may hold promise, but not for a woman with friends and a life in London."

How nice to hear him echo her own points from before the general's announcement. "Correct in all aspects, my lord. So you shall simply have to accompany me."

Stanley sputtered, most ungentlemanly, and Cara loved that she could so break his composure. A quick glance showed that Althorp derived unseemly glee from her routing the other lord. He acted far too pleased for a man who'd also spent the past two days dealing her out of the London game.

"No, no," she said, saving Stanley from needing to reply. "An unmarried woman couldn't travel alone with a man and two servants. How very unseemly. Since you're already wed, you'd be right out." She turned her grin on Althorp. "How about it, Al? Would you marry me and adventure into the Americas?"

They should all have laughed off her mocking suggestion, fair play for the way she'd been treated since arriving in the general's domain. But no merriment or derision followed her invitation. Althorp nervously pulled his dark, silky hair forward over his shoulder, fiddling with it. His fingers continued to thread through the strands in her periphery as he locked his gaze to hers.

He scrutinized her as if judging all her actions and motives up till this point, and Cara held her breath, wondering if she would pass his inspection and retain his friendship. As long moments passed, she grew overwarm under his intense regard. Had she ever been the subject of such ardent attention? She had half a mind to apologize for her comment, but didn't truly believe doing so would change the atmosphere. Hopefully, her friend would find whatever he needed.

Suddenly, Althorp was beside her. He grabbed both her hands in his own. His low voice carried through the whole, hushed room when he said, "If you'll have me in truth, I'll pledge to you today."

Struck dumb, Cara felt a flush creep up her body, starting at their conjoined hands and traveling up her arm into her heart. This wasn't how her afternoon—her life— was meant to play out. She'd no inkling that his affection ran so deep and had never let herself consider a true relationship with any man she'd met in London. Where Stanley had been a bit of ill-conceived fun, Al had been completely off-limits, a skeet flush in a seven-card game.

She couldn't think while Al's thumbs drew idle diamonds and clubs on her knuckles. Utterly thrown by the turn of events, she snatched her hands back, trying not to see the crestfallen expression on his face as his eyes finally dropped away from hers.

She breathed deeply, trying to regain her equilibrium. True, they'd quickly become friends. True, they shared cards and a sense of otherness. True, she found joy in his respectfully platonic company. But could that support a foundation of marital relations? Would he expect her to become a lady of the *haut monde*? Would his family even allow a union with a common gambler of dubious purity?

She couldn't deny his handsome features. The strong nose matching his strong shoulders and active spirit. His near-black hair, the kind that half-penny novelists spent pages running a heroine's fingers through. He had a quiet capability about him, too, that had her approaching him for advice in all the foreign situations she'd recently experienced. While she knew his virile attraction and that she could count on him in all her contemporary crises, she remained unsure of her interest in trading her life in London for that of a married woman. Even a woman married to her well-formed friend.

Although, what kept her now from marriage as an institution? It could simply be that she'd never met a man she could stand for extensive lengths of time; in which case, Althorp made a handsome change. Or perhaps her prior distaste had more to do with the fact that husbands did not approve of gambler-wives. But Althorp enjoyed matching her at the card table and already accepted her as his superior in that endeavor, gracefully folding before her prowess when his allowance ran thin.

Perhaps they could make a go of that Washoe game together. Certainly, she'd miss him if she went alone. She'd undoubtedly want to share her wonder at the territories and her glee when she became the uncontested high-stakes champion on multiple continents.

The general cleared his throat. "Don't decide too quickly, miss. Lord Greenhope can't yet be discounted."

Cara checked her contemplation of her friend's positive qualities. For all she'd been dissecting Al, doing the same for Stanley never crossed her mind. Once she'd opened herself to the possibility of marital bliss, her illicit lover somehow folded out of the picture. They'd enjoyed sharing their bodies, yes, but Stanley had never matched her at poker, nor elsewhere outside the bedroom. Maybe when he'd been younger he might have, before he stopped adventuring. Besides, divorce would be near-impossible, and she didn't much care to be called *mistress.*

Wait. If he could be on the marriage market, then—

"What's happened, man?" the marquis demanded of their host. "Tell me at once!"

The general shifted a bit until he reached military attention. "My apologies, my lord. 'Twas an unfortunate jest." He *hemmed.* "Now for the bad news out of London, I'm afraid. The Lady Greenhope perished in the same murder as Miss St. Cross's adversaries."

Stanley stilled, undoubtedly frozen with shock. The poor man. While he'd been off rescuing her, the same threat ended his own wife's time on Earth.

"I must return to London," he said, "to put affairs in order."

Cara stroked his arm, uncaring for propriety. "I'm sorry for your loss."

He shook her off. "Don't be. She was never faithful and always more interested in social position than in me. But she was still my wife, my responsibility. I need to get home."

The general led him out, calling for horses.

Only Al remained with her in the room. He watched the fireplace, orange flames giving his profile a heavenly glow. She only needed so many signs.

"So, Al, will you marry me and join me in the territories?" Her ribs contracted and a fluttering obstructed her throat. She couldn't take the words back now. He'd indicated a willingness before, but that happed ere he'd taken the chance to think it through, before he'd known she might reject him so callously.

A slightly hysterical laugh escaped him, and once again he spun her in happy circles. Then his lips met hers, and she knew in her bones she'd won the largest pot with her daring.

Their breaths mingled, and she melted into his strong frame. He matched her so perfectly, able to take her weight but not attempting to wrest control of the soft presses and nibbles. She lost long moments in his embrace before they pulled apart.

"Yes. I'll marry you tonight."

EPILOGUE

8 months later

Cara pulled out another sheet of stationary and a bulb pen. This last thank-you letter after the wedding struck her as the most difficult, and—truthfully—she'd been putting it off.

Dearest Stanley,

No. That pushed all bounds of propriety. Especially now that she'd married another man, a fellow of his Club nonetheless. She needed something else, a salutation by turns both formal and affectionate.

My Dear Lord Greenhope,
We should like to express our deepest thanks for your Thoughtful Gift. While Lady Althorp no longer wears such accoutrements, the Exquisite detailing and tailored shape make the Delicate Item a perfect memento of our time together in London.

Which said, in its stilted way, that the improved mechanical penis Stanley had sent made a silly gag gift, but a friendly one. They appreciated it as a symbol of his blessings and best wishes for their new life together, and for the fairytale beauty it spun around the old life that involved all three of them.

Of course, he might have expected her to continue masquerading as a technical-gentleman in order to smooth her way in the male-dominated territories. But out in Washoe, no man would dare tell a woman what she could or couldn't do. There existed no gentlemen-only clubs.

Cara thought back to the day the Cross Your Heart was completed. Al had engaged only local workmen, endearing the pair of them to the populace before they'd even finished settling in; and he'd also been a sporadic presence on the site, helping to raise walls and holding whatever needed holding.

So when the last nail wanted hammering, the construction foreman passed the tool to the highly-involved owner. Al immediately handed the hammer to his wife, knowing that she'd want to be part of this historic moment.

Unlike she'd expect in England, no one had rushed to remove the heavy implement from her hand. No one seemed disturbed that a woman might wield the bludgeon. After all, this far west, numerous members of her sex had involved themselves in building their own houses, barns, and fences. On these uncharted plains, no reasonable worker refrained from effort.

That day, she put away her chrome cock for good. For all that she'd been airily wearing the gowns of her former life, pre-London, while they'd waited for the building's erection—and how lucky that colonial fashions seemed a year or two behind—she'd always anticipated her legal manhood's reemergence. But not from that day forward.

Finally, she was free to be the woman she'd always wanted to be.

More than that, she had a gaming house all her own. One where her tastes directed the game and players always made room for her at the table. No more worrying about where she'd go next or whether the pot would be worth it.

And no more loneliness. She'd never considered herself lonely. She simply hadn't sought out human companionship, preferring to hunt her passion. Now, though, she had Mindy as both a dealer and security sharpshooter, Nathan as her hotel manager, and the inimitable Lord Althorp as her husband.

She fought off a flush as she recalled what happened *after* she'd nailed the last board in place and the vendors had cleared out. Unfurnished, the new establishment was no place yet for patrons and players, but it was hers. Cara and Al had intended to give themselves a tour, but ended up going from stunned awe that they owned this whole place to inescapable desire.

She flung herself at him, still taking in the glorious woodcut ceilings, and captured his attention with her ardent kiss. Even after months of happy familiarity, their bodies held a pitch of excitement whenever they came together. He took no pause to get his mind in the game, pulling her impossibly closer as their laughing mouths slanted together. They clung to one another, joy and love coursing through their veins.

In bare moments, Al had removed her corset and shift with their months' practice, and she'd wrangled his jacket and tie to the unswept floor. Just as she contemplated pushing her beloved husband against the door to get some leverage, regardless of whether the remaining workmen outside might notice the noise, Althorp tumbled her to the ground. She let out a surprised giggle which only grew stronger as he tangled himself in her skirts, unable to remove those as easily as the rest of her ensemble.

Lord, when had she last giggled during sex?

Somehow, they emerged naked from their disarrangement. Her giggles faded away, and a silent agreement passed between them: that this was good, that they belonged here, that all was right in the world, that they'd live this happily for the rest of their lives.

Unable to bear the soul-deep seriousness anymore, Cara wrapped a bare leg around his hips, pulling him closer atop her and squirming to spur him on. Though her own motions had caused their alignment, she paused for a shocked moment, enjoying the heat of him that blanketed her from shoulder to junction. They *fit* perfectly, as no one had ever matched her before. She clutched him hard for a moment, all skin and muscle locked together, then loosed her arms.

Al took full advantage of his freedom, leaning back on his perch to feast his gaze on her naked form. "Whatever hand I may someday play, no stakes could ever match the prize I already hold." He clung to her sides with warm hands, giving no quarter to the idea that he should ever lose her in a future match.

Her eyes fluttered shut against such unhidden emotion, and she gasped in a desperate breath as he set to enflaming her every sense. His fingers trailed her stomach and thighs till she twitched and whimpered to get his touch into a more intimate place. He leaned forward to nibble at the crook of her neck and then down to the top of her breast, but never traveling further.

She arched and writhed and gasped, but she couldn't let his frustrating attentions go unmatched. No, she gave as much pleasure as she took, delighting in his every panting breath and groaning sigh. Though in a less advantageous position for free reign of his body, she used what leverage she had to suck at his earlobe and run firm hands over his back and chest, even between his balls.

Unspoken, they broke from their mutual teasing to push themselves together in that most friendly of ways, until he was seated fully inside of her. They paused to bask in warmth and newly familiar awe. Then she dug her heel into his lower back, and the moment ended in thrusting waves of unending ardor.

She tensed and released around him, making them both breathless with the pleasure of it. They strained together, needing to be closer—to each other and to that perfect peak. She knew just how to hold her hand under the smooth hair at his nape to drive him that little bit wilder. He knew just the angle to press her higher.

Untamed now, they joined at a frenzied pace, then collapsed together to the bare floor that would someday sport tables and chairs.

He maneuvered them onto their sides, running soothing strokes over her hip, gentling her through the aftershocks. "By God, I love you, Crossy," he said when their hearts had calmed and they simply lay on their discarded clothes in that empty front room. "You're the best part of my recall to England."

He still called her *Crossy*, much to the confusion of anyone who heard him do it, since her name no longer bore any resemblance to *St. Cross.* Colonials sometimes had trouble remembering *Lady*, but they certainly knew her as *Althorp.*

She snuggled into his embrace, eyes on the future location of their bar, their dream. "I love you, too. I never expected to marry a titled man or start a new life in the far colonies, but I'm glad I did. With you."

Lord Althorp and I are doing well, and look forward to any visits. Though you must promise not to let the viscount's parents know how much he enjoys tending the bar at Cross Your Heart. They'd be Appalled to learn of his publican shifts. No remaining solely a financial investor for this gentleman!

They'd never intended to call their club Cross Your Heart. The gentle pun had been a reference only. They'd intended to come up with something else later—perhaps *The Caller Club 2.* But someone in town had heard the name and gifted them with the sign. Now she couldn't think of anything more perfect.

I'm starting to learn Spanish and a few words in the languages spoken by the Natives. Soon enough, we'll be true Members of the Community. Oh! Last week, the territorial governor came to my backroom high-stakes table. Usually, Lord Althorp and I don't bother to hold a private game, preferring to join the common room play-ers, but we finally met with another Extravagant Gambler. The governor knocked my husband right out of the game, but I managed to hold the table and to Restore our Honor.

Tu amiga para siempre,
Lady Cara Althorp, née St. Cross

The Victoriana Centuries

Or, the 19th & 20th Centuries

THE CLOCKWORK DANCER

Carlotta finished her combination—*en pointe* and *arabesque!*—and marked her landing position against Alexander, her *premier danseur noble.* No, Carlotta thought, he was still too far away. She'd have to change the choreography to put him further downstage by the start of the second movement or to put Beatrice, the *prima ballerina,* closer to him.

She scribbled these last notes into her choreography journal, then tossed it onto the creaking table, its three-legged chair the only other furniture in her bare warehouse-cum-studio. She walked back across the room to grab Alexander, then dragged him along and reposi-tioned him next to his *corps de ballet.*

Nothing could look more beautiful: her own ballet troupe, all perfectly aligned and technically exact. They shone in glistening gold and steel and brass, the long, basket-like lines of their outer weavings flowing in curves and rounded spaces that hinted at their streamlined dance quality. Someday, she would give them faces and features made of putty, but for now they remained unabashedly technological, a comment on the dancer in modern society. Someday, she'd have a real company willing to attempt her moves, moves not always classical or neoclassical, but modern and eastern and strange due to periodic clockwork stops—actually harder for the clockwork troupe to execute, because they had to start up again after stuttering.

She wiped Alexander down, he being the only creation she'd worked with today. "I'll be back tomorrow with your drinks, everyone." The ensemble didn't answer, of course, and she didn't expect them to. She knew they were simply metal and bolts and powder batteries. Until she inserted their program cards, they remained pretty statues. That didn't keep her from talking to them, though, as to a pet or an automotive cab.

Carlotta put her outdoor clothes on over the foundation garments she'd worked in. First the ecru linen shirt, mended in many places, then her dark woolen skirt and the leather waist-cincher that was her only nod to fashion. All drab, all not nearly modish. But if she had to choose between a new shirt or another month's rent on her warehouse, she'd choose the studio every time.

Outside, she locked the brick building's rusting door with several padlocks. If she lost her company, she'd have nothing. At a brisk walk, she made it to High Street before businesses started to close. She had yet to purchase the special oil for her ensemble, and it was already Thursday. They had a performance the next night.

"Hello, Miss Stembridge," the establishment's owner greeted. "I held this can back for you."

She thanked him and produced her payment. In moments, she walked out the door with a brown bag holding her sole acquisition.

"Excuse me," an unfamiliar voice said from behind her. Carlotta turned to see a tall man who looked to be in his mid-twenties and who possessed a pair of well-defined thighs, visible even through his trousers. His long nose was as pointed as a piece of wire, and his fine-spun cotton shirt gave an impression of moderate means. But the outdoors had left its mark on his tanned skin. *Not wealthy enough to be a patron.*

He caught her arm with an elongated grace, as though she'd stumbled, and his eyebrows flew into his shock of dark hair as though he couldn't believe he'd just touched her. "I'm terribly sorry, but I saw one of your ballets last month. Your choreography!" He paused dramatically, and she identified him as a bit silly, if well meaning. "Your choreography astounded me with its complexity and emotion."

A figurant or a student of the arts, he must be. Her heart beat faster at praise from a knowledgeable member of her public. "Thank you, sir. You're too kind." She waited a moment in silence, hoping he'd say something else. Someone so handsome, so graceful, and so interested in her ballet... she didn't want the conversation to end so soon.

He shuffled his feet and looked down at the concrete stoop, giving her a good look at his dark, chin-length crop. "I—I'm Henry, by the way. Pleased to make your acquaintance, Miss Stembridge."

How charming! "Carlotta, please," she reassured him. She wondered what movement that hair might make when a hand, perhaps hers, set it to swinging.

He smiled at her, and opened his posture into second position. "Allow me, Miss Carlotta," he said, swooping down to whisk away her package. "I shall be happy to escort you through these rough neighborhoods."

Shoppers bustled past them on the street, putting paid to his description. She giggled, and took back her appropriated oil. "I'm glad to meet you, Henry, but I don't let strange men walk me home."

"I'm not strange!" he protested, pulling a face like an actor in a pantomime. He grasped her hand, his manner reminiscent of a character in a Haymarket opera. "Then say you'll dine with me tomorrow. I simply must see you again."

Who was she to deny a handsome, learned man who appreciated her ballets over her other charms? A woman of commitments, that was who. While she'd love to oblige him, she did have other engagements. "Perhaps another time, Henry." She could almost taste his disappointment, but teasing would be unsuitable to a straightforward personality like her own. "Tomorrow night, my troupe dances at the *Follies of Fancy.* Will you be attending the performance?"

He was gratifyingly quick to request all the details. "I look forward to it, Miss Carlotta." Then he strode off, his long legs extending in a perfectly even gait.

* * *

Carlotta arranged her dancers under a drop cloth next to the unsanded stageboards. She checked the order of her program cards a final time and reinserted them into her troupe. Her mind was everywhere today, everywhere but on her work. First she'd mislaid the oil, and then she'd forgotten the order she'd fed Alexander his programs and had to start over. Not to mention the moment when Beatrice plunged into the illusionist's rehearsal. She hadn't realized she'd given Beatrice any programs at all!

Her mind had flitted off on tangents. She noticed the slender shoulders of a stage hand and thought of sweet Henry stooping to carry her shopping. She caught a glimpse of well-formed ankle from the burlesque dancers who preceded her troupe on stage, and she wondered about the exact shape of Henry's ankles; she knew he walked in perfect alignment, but she didn't know the exact play of bone and sinew.

Would he come tonight? And did she want him to? She thought of the burlesque dancers again and half-hoped he'd miss the performance. Her ambitions and talents were reduced to this. *This.* Her creative soul was sandwiched between a burlesque troupe and a pair of mimes.

But she was on her way up. She had to be.

"Oh, Carlotta!" Sandy bustled up beside her and began hanging strips of fabric in easy reach of the stage. She was a rounded, red-haired woman who organized costumes for the burlesquers. "Have you seen the audience tonight?" Sandy had a giant heart, a willing hand with the needle, and always the best gossip.

"Any patrons of the arts for the courting?" Carlotta asked, half-serious.

Leaning in, Sandy stage-whispered, "One of the great society lords is out there. I think Henry brought him. Sweet boy."

"Henry?" Not *her* Henry, surely. Her Henry with the thick, dark hair and the unspeakably coordinated legs.

Sandy gasped with melodramatic relish. Her next words were sure to contain some nuggets of both truthful gossip and sensational rumormongering. "You haven't met Henry yet? You'll adore him. He dances, I think, but only as a hobby. He's something of a fanatic about our romantic way of life, you see. Too bad he doesn't appear to have any money." She paused to swish a faded silk scarf through the air, checking its quality of movement before stuffing it into her costume bag and taking out another. "Though, if he's managed to bring a moneyed lord with him, he might have useful connections after all."

With that intriguing description, Sandy dashed off to fix costumes in the opposite wings. Left to her own devices, Carlotta peeked through the curtain, hunting in the audience to catch a glimpse of the alleged sumptuously attired lord. She wasn't looking for her Henry in particular. Not at all. She was looking for a potential patron so she could put on her own extravaganzas *and* pay her warehouse's rent.

But she made out only lights and outlines. The audience could have been made of mechanicals, for all she could see.

* * *

After the revue crashed to an end, the artists and well-wishers congregated in front of the main entrance on a patch of concrete that served as a foyer. The stage and the benches took up almost all the interior space at the theatre, so artists and performers had to meet friends and patrons at the doors. Carlotta knew a number of less-scrupulous creators who chose to use the back alley, with all its darker connotations, a source to which she would never stoop.

She searched the milling crowd for a glimpse of the supposedly moneyed man. *Over there!* Did she spy a brocade waistcoat? No, but the wearer had a cotton-muslin shirt reminiscent of the linen Henry had worn when he'd enquired after her schedule. Much as she enjoyed watching her ballets performed, in retrospect she could have bowed out of this performance in favor of letting him take her on an outing. They could have discussed dance in the modern consciousness, the lines of a building as compared to *port de bras* in second position.

"Ar-herm." A throat cleared at her side, the sound cutting the moist air.

Carlotta startled. *It's him! The moneyed lord!* He was an older man with graying hair that didn't detract from his aristocratic bearing. Too old for the military, he still carried himself well, his wide shoulders pulling at the severe dress coat he wore. She couldn't help but think his metal-sharp nose looked a lot like Henry's.

Now is not the time to dwell on a young gentleman. Focus on the patron. "Good evening, sir. I hope you enjoyed the show."

He dipped his head in brief acknowledgement, but spared no syllables for niceties. "I'm told those coordinated automatons are your creation," he said.

He wanted to speak about her dance troupe! This might be the break she'd needed all these long months. She made an affirmative noise just as her Henry appeared at the lord's side.

Today Henry looked different, older and richer, with a velvet waistcoat that played in the dangerous field between ridiculous and fashion-setting. He also looked harried, harassed, and ready to leave. Henry hadn't seen her yet, so she observed him more frankly than she might otherwise.

Henry addressed the moneyed lord. "Please, Father, let's end this evening."

Father? Carlotta looked up and sideways to slyly catalogue Henry's handsome features and compare them against her potential patron's.

"If you'll excuse me for a moment," the older gentleman said to Carlotta. Then he turned to his son—*his son!*—with a tightening mouth. "Perhaps if you did your duty and took an interest in the Lady Anne, this evening could be considered successful. As it cannot, you will entertain your guest while I discuss important matters with this tink—inventor."

Carlotta was too busy mentally molding a putty face that looked like Henry—for her dancers, of course—to take offence at the old man's slip. He'd almost called her a *tinker*. And would that be so bad? Not from her point of view, certainly, but if it kept him from financing her enterprises, then she'd need to convince him of her ladylike qualities. She smoothed her faded skirts and schooled her expression into proper English stoicism.

Henry saw her now, following his father's lead. He bent over her hand. "Miss Carlotta. A pleasure to see you again."

Their eyes met as he stood, and she felt heat running through her like oil. It loosened her body as it slid down and pooled in her stomach. Her cheeks trembled with the effort to suppress an overlarge smile.

"Father, I'd like to introduce Miss Carlotta Stembridge, the choreographer and creator of tonight's ballet. Miss Stembridge, allow me to introduce my father, Lord Rodger, Earl of Mulbrendon." Henry might have said something else but was soon cut off.

"Ah, Lord Henry." The speaker was an unexpectedly tall woman, with her hair piled atop her head like a contrived birds' nest and a satin gown much too fine for the *Follies.*

Henry shot his eyes to Carlotta, making an apologetic half-shrug in her direction before greeting the newcomer. "Lady Anne. I thought I'd lost you."

The lady smirked, but quickly smoothed her expression. "It's lucky, then, that I found myself. And who is this sweet girl?"

Carlotta bristled at being termed a *sweet girl,* but she had to admire the lady's technique. She'd firmly placed Carlotta in a lower tier, not only socially but also in maturity. The lady clearly brooked no competition.

She hoped Henry might stand up for her honor, but instead it was his father who explained. "This talented inventor crafted those metal men who so enchanted us all." The conversation now returned to its original track. "I was quite impressed by your abilities, Miss Stembridge."

"Thank you, my lord." Now she simply needed to steer the topic to patron-age. *Simply, hah!*

"Have you thought about the military applications of such metal men?" He gestured now to where Alexander posed next to a young girl for a daguerreotype.

The evening lights glinted off Alexander's long lines. The young girl beside him didn't appear to be moving his arm in any way, yet the articulated fingers seemed to curve naturally around her shoulder. Carlotta was sure that if she moved closer, she could see who was posing her dancer. Perhaps the girl's father...?

"I can't say that I have, my lord." She stifled a giggle at the image of an army of metal men *glissade en avant* across a battlefield, neatly leaping over any obstacles. Not that there had been any major conflicts in recent memory. "The programs for something so structured as a ballet require a complexity that would not translate to the vagaries of the battlefield as I understand them." She expected the nobleman to ignore her expert opinion. After all, she was but a choreographer and a civilian.

"I appreciate your clear thinking, Miss Stembridge," he said. "However, I'm certain we could work something out, if you'd only be willing to engage in some research."

In her peripheral vision, Carlotta saw Lady Anne take Henry's arm, fondling the luxe fabric that covered it. "Let's leave your father to deal with the tradeswoman."

Henry shook her off and took Carlotta's right hand in both of his. "Please don't think ill of me, Miss Carlotta." The heat of his hands, Carlotta thought wistfully, imparted the desperation of his heart. "I look forward to our next meeting. We had agreed upon tomorrow, had we not?"

Had they? She didn't recall their setting a time for any sort of assignation. Still, the fact that he spoke so boldly and openly proved his desire to spend time with *her*, not the Lady Anne. But did she wish to embroil herself in a family squabble? To stand betwixt the man who believed in her choreography and his lord father who thought she should throw over dance for armament?

Yes. "Tomorrow will be acceptable, Lord Henry." She made him a half-bow, half-curtsey, then turned to his father. "I'm afraid I'm not available for military contracts, Lord Rodger. However, if you find yourself in need of a choreographer, please do get in touch." To the Lady Anne she made a full bow. "My lady."

Goodbyes complete, the power entirely hers, she swept back inside the theatre, making for the backstage area. Her knees wobbled and her heart pounded so hard she could feel its beat in her elbows. Had she really just dismissed a lord, an earl? A grin wended its way across her face. She had, indeed. And nothing bad had happened at all.

* * *

She put Alexander back in his proper place in her warehouse and produced a soft cotton cloth. "I met the most wonderful man," she told the company while she rubbed at their outer forms. The telling made her giddy, and near-hysteric laughter burst from her mouth. "He's a dancer and a gentleman. When did we last meet one of those?" Conscientiously, she rubbed a second coat of oil into each dancer's inner gears. They'd done wonderful work the night before, gaining the attention of a real lord, albeit one who wanted them for a separate purpose.

"And he likes me. He wants to see me tonight. Isn't it wonderful?" She spun in a *pirouette*, then into an *arabesque*, a sweep forward, *tour jeté*, and *pirouette* again. "He likes our work," she whispered to the dancers. "It's marvelous."

Alexander's left arm hadn't glided as smoothly as she'd have liked last night, so she gave that rotary an extra cleaning. *Whirrrr-click!* went Alexander's inner shoulder. Carlotta frowned and leaned in, then put pressure on the circumgyrator. Again, the whirring noise stuttered up, and this time Alexander's arm moved in an ever-halting arc that terminated on contact with her head.

She wouldn't give him the satisfaction of saying "Ouch!" Instead, she said, "Hmmmm," and reached through his endoskeleton to remove the offending gear and attached box. The problem fit easily into her palm, but proved its technical difficulty when it continued to whir and click. She'd removed it from Alexander's body and from his power source, but still the piece shuddered on her hand. Curious, yes—and its actions ruined the fluid serenity of her choreography.

She slipped the recalcitrant stuff into her purse, vowing to fix it after her rendezvous with Lord Henry. She jumped into her layers of clothing, a firm believer in *when in doubt, go big.* Even simple clothes looked grand when you wore them one atop the other, longest skirts underneath the shortest and full sleeves creating a bell effect when cinched by summer's armbands. As for the unfurling hems and ragged edges, they became a fashionable jumble, whereas they'd tell a sorry tale if seen one at a time. A pinch to her cheeks, and she grabbed her purse on the way out the door.

Outside, she started in on her numerous locks, when Henry's deep voice sounded behind her, causing her to fumble the keys. "Hello, Miss Carlotta." He scooped them up and passed them back. "You look lovely this evening. A true vision before my eyes."

She felt the blush starting in her cheeks and forced herself to make eye contact, noting his dapper top hat. She hoped she'd dressed appropriately. "Where are we going?"

He offered her the crook of his arm and held his limb with strength and precision. Yes, he definitely had some dance training. "I thought we could make a tour of it," he said. His muscles tremored for a moment, then firmed again as he led her down the steps to an automotive cabriolet. She tried not to think how the Lady Anne had laid her fingers in the exact same spot the night before.

The cabriolet was painted a smooth black over what she knew was a polished bronze structure. The long nose ended in a squiggle, the auxiliary crank, and the rear-hinged doors opened with chromium knobs. Her fingers trailed over citrine silk when Henry helped her inside, and she rubbed her fingertips back and forth over the lining to experience the full effect.

"I've never undertaken to motor in such a carriage," she said to explain her fascination. *Indeed*, she thought wryly, *perhaps I expected to motor in such a carriage only in the presence of an undertaker.*

He turned coal-black eyes towards her, and her heart beat uptempo. His eyes peeked through floppy hair, making him seem both sensitive and mysterious at once. She settled her skirts as best she could, but they overlapped his trousers in the close confines of the cab.

Procuring a basket from somewhere, Henry began to plate a full supper. "These sprouts are from America, brought in fresh by steamer this morning. And the juice is straight from Andalucía, kept refrigerated on the silver train."

She hid a grin beneath her hand at his pride in such a modern meal. Her breakfasts and suppers daily consisted of the same brown porridge; any change would be a treat, even the simple pleasure of his company. "I'm quite impressed," she said, and his shoulders acquired a jaunty tilt.

For an hour, they drove the city, past the steamworks, through the seedy area where the Garment District bordered Little Orient, and around the city park. By the time they reached the Season residences of the lords and ladies, the wine had made her slightly tipsy, and she leaned against Henry, holding his hand.

A sad breath escaped him, fogging the window that framed the twinkling gaslamps. "You, Carlotta, are everything I've ever wanted in love and in life."

And what of the Lady Anne? Your father clearly approves of her. She snuggled closer into him. "You shouldn't say that so despondently. I've grown quite fond of you too, you know. You needn't worry on that score."

His hand tightened on hers. "It's been so wonderful these few days. Meeting you at long last, taking you on the town. Everything I've ever wanted." He buried his nose in her hair, and she gasped at the ticklish sensation from his breaths. "You shine so brightly," he murmured, almost too low for her to hear. "Your pure *boheme* radiates through your art."

She shivered, but didn't pull away. "Would you like to see the inner workings of my studio?"

He nodded against her neck, and she tapped the partition to let the driver know their destination. Henry stayed wrapped up around her, and she didn't have the heart to disengage him. At first, she excused herself: his childlike cuddling oughtn't be disturbed. But when his palms rubbed slowly over her arms and imparted their warmth, she admitted to herself that she let him stay because she liked it.

She liked the feel of him, his long muscles giving off heat and his gentle caresses making her skin sparkle. She liked that he felt so at ease with her, that he trusted her enough to go wherever she decreed. She liked how much he liked her.

Carlotta tucked one of her arms around him, completing the clutch and, not coincidentally, smoothing his hands over her back rather than her arms. Now she heard his heartbeat and fancied herself ensconced in his embrace, ready to emerge as a young butterfly. That might make a good theme for another ballet. *Hmmm.*

They tumbled breathlessly from the cabriolet, neither holding balance on usually stable feet, hanging on to their closeness. At the door of her warehouse, Carlotta freed herself partially from Henry's arms, shuddering at the renewed cold. She pressed the door open and moved forward gracelessly, Henry molded against her back while she led him to a pile of costumes in the corner. Not, perhaps, the softest bed, but surely the easiest and the most bohemian.

They tumbled to the ground, glad to be steady and intimately entwined. Henry's tongue glided lightly over her jugular, gently, gently, surprising a whine from her throat. Who knew her neck was so sensitive? She'd wrapped so many rough scarves around it during the winter months.

Henry lapped the vein once again, then levered himself up on an elbow. "Do you have anything?"

No, she didn't. She hadn't expected such an ardent suit this evening, hadn't needed a method of preventing pregnancy in so long. All the same, she groped for her reticule. Perhaps it hid some contrivance?

Henry unlaced her cincher while she rummaged through the pouch. *No, no. Maybe.* In her hand, Carlotta held Alexander's scapula and the attached circumgyrator. Of its own volition, the broken motor started to purr. "Perhaps," she suggested, holding out the curved square, "we can 'trundle' like the Americans."

Henry snatched the piece from her hands and slipped her chemise from her shoulders. She took that as agreement and reveled in his forcefulness, hidden behind that so-polite exterior she'd experienced over the last two days.

Reclining against the costumes, Carlotta focused on his fingers as they pulled and unbuttoned, revealing more of her own paleness as well as his darker skin. She bit her lip and kept herself from reaching out. Henry clearly had a plan, and she wouldn't interrupt it for the world, for a theatre manager, for the patronage of a wealthy *balletomane.*

Henry arranged the scapula analogue against her *mons,* its curve pressing lightly into her pretty thing. The piece stuttered against her, motor unreliable, and her hips jumped at the unexpected vibration. Henry's free hand stroked her belly briefly, a calming touch, before he reached for the silk of his ascot and bound the metal against her.

He sat back on his heels between her legs, surveying his handiwork, and Carlotta barely kept herself from squirming against the light tremors on her most secret lips. "Ingenious, my dear," he said, then thumbed the attached circumgyrator.

She arched at the increased strength and speed of the pulsations that moved up from the crux of her legs, through the core of her soul, and into her fast-beating heart. "Yes," she hissed.

And then the sensation was gone. *No!* The blasted thing didn't get to break now! She opened her eyes—when had she closed them?—and witnessed Henry's smug grin. He'd flipped the motor off.

She growled at him, only half playful, but he didn't relent. Very carefully, he avoided changing the setting or providing any pressure when he bowed his body over hers. His tongue peeked out, and she hoped he'd return to her neck or lave a nipple or work his way down her stomach and pick up the buzzer's slack.

He didn't. Softly, oh so softly, he drew figures on her right breast with his tongue. On her left, his thumb moved with barely any force, rubbing at the place where her breast met her ribcage over and over, never varying into a more solid caress, nor letting up. She strained upwards, trying to get more touch, more pressure.

But with every flex of her spine, he moved back to keep the constant graze. "So perfect," he whispered. "Everything I've ever wanted." He punctuated the statement by turning on the motor again, at the lowest setting.

She screamed her pleasure at the thrum, then sobbed a breath. It wasn't enough. It couldn't be enough. The light touches, the glancing strokes... did he mean to keep her in stand-by mode all evening? She'd never survive!

As if taking pity on her, Henry removed his too-gentle hand from her breast and brought it between her legs to rest against the vibrating gold. *Yes!,* she begged him, *push against it.* Again, he ignored her internal command, preferring to tease and test. He left his hand against the plate, unmoving, and exhaled hot air against her nipple.

On his third exhale, she squirmed just right and managed to find an angle that pushed her center against the piece with each pulse of her hips. Her cries grew faster between desperate breaths, and all at once he crushed her against the long lines of his body.

Their mouths clashed and chests met. His erection pressed hard and strong against the ascot-wrapped toy from jewels to tip, driving it closer to her body and then taking it away again in a rhythm that he alone could control.

She shook under him and wrapped her legs around his back, drawing on her own flexibility and physique to pull him closer with each forward movement. And then he flipped the rotor, setting the scapula to maximal energy.

Her whole body quivered at the tickling tension, and Henry came with a roar and a splash of semen against her belly. *Just like a man,* she thought, even as she gasped aloud at the sensation of his weight holding down the re-verberator. She loved the pressure. She wanted it closer, *please, closer,* and maybe filling an emptiness that she didn't quite understand. At the same time, it needed to stop. If she were alone, she'd stop now. She didn't want any more. Her head twisted from side to side, and she bit into Henry's elbow when it came in range.

In a different interpretation than she'd intended, he picked himself up and went back to his pre-orgasmic mo-tions, but with more more more. One thumb flicked a nipple back and forth, while his other hand massaged the undulating piece against her. Harder, softer. Forward, backward. Sometimes in tight circles that he would match on her nipple.

She felt her completion building, and her hips moved mindlessly. Carlotta couldn't match his hand's rhythm. She could barely think enough to keep breathing. Her arms flailed about her. When he bent to bite at her nipple and then lave it with a much rougher tongue than before, she pulled him close with one grasping fist and tried to push him away with the other.

He removed his hand from the junction of her thighs, much to her dismay, but replaced it with his athletic thigh. He drove the leg upwards, and she drove herself down and around. Wanting, needing, hoping, biting. *So close!*

With a last nudge of his limb, the vibration against her secret pushed her over the edge into the highest level she'd ever attained. She felt her blood chasing through her clenching veins, as the constant shuddering drew her into ecstasy. She howled her impossible delight, unable to escape the sweet pulses from within and without, writhing in her desire for more... and less.

She knocked him away and whined—words would form eventually—for him to disengage the device. With one last caressing shiver, Henry unwound his ascot and removed its bounty.

Exhausted, she slumped against the costumes and wrapped her arms around her new lover. She'd keep him.

* * *

Carlotta woke up warm and in shadowy quietude. She squinted at looming shadows with glinting knives at the ready, and her hand flew to her throat. *What are those?*

Oh. Her mind caught up to the rest of her. Without lights, she hadn't recognized her studio and its clockwork denizens. A warm hand traversed her hip to press flat against her stomach in a lazy cuddle. "It's nothing," she reassured her sleeping companion, regretful that she'd woken him.

He pressed up against her back, all warm muscle and sense memory of the night before. Hot air caressed her ear. "Then let's spend the day right here, enjoying one another until I must leave." He nipped her earlobe. "You were magnificent."

She turned in his arms to ruffle his hair. "Right here? All day on my floor?"

"I can't think of any place I'd rather be." His voice husked where hers teased, and he brought her over to his way of thinking with his lips, giving her a long, slick frisson of pleasure.

She sighed into his mouth, contented. "You don't have to leave on my account," she offered. "I know it's not much, but... " *No, he won't want to share my warehouse.* Henry had swept her off her feet like a heroine in a penny dreadful, but that didn't make him her lifelong companion. The world didn't work that way. And she certainly couldn't compete with the moneyed ladies of his other world.

He brushed her mouth with his again, then pulled away. "It's everything I've ever dreamed of," he said seriously, his hands coming to her shoulders so that he could look directly into her eyes. "A life of art with a virtuoso like you. I wouldn't leave if I mustn't, but," he paused. "What was that?"

"What was what?" She wasn't going to let him out of this conversation for such an obvious contrivance.

Clank. Whirr-click.

"That."

Click-drag-clank. Clank-drag-click.

She hunted through the shadows on the floor, and Henry scrambled up. He positioned himself between her and the noise with all the chivalry that lordly aristocrats proclaimed. *There!* She flicked the trigger on the gaslamp, bathing the room in growing yellow light as one lamp's ignition triggered the next, and so on, till all were lit.

Stillness. Silence. No one moved, no one spoke. But Alexander stood in the center of the floor. She must have left a card in the night before. No matter. Henry didn't get to change the subject. "So, if you don't want to leave, why should you? You could stay here and dance for me. I'd love to have a real *premier danseur noble.*" She could picture it: Henry and Beatrice dancing her ballet, flying across stages and perineums throughout Europe while ecstatic sponsors offered her their congratulations and their bursaries.

Click-drag-clank.

Alexander bore down directly on them. He shouldn't be able to. This section of the room always stood for "the audience." *Chasse* front right, *chasse* front left. Ever closer and closer. Directly in front of Henry now, Alexander moved into a *pirouette.*

"No!" she cried as she saw Alexander's leg moving forward into fourth position. That was no simple *pirouette.* It was about to become a *fouetté rond de jambe en tournant,* a solid whipping kick in and out while turning. With Alexander's metal frame, Henry stood in the way of an industrial grinder.

But Henry, too, had some skill on the stage, and he spotted the move in time. He whisked her off the ground and leapt out of the way. Less graceful than Alexander, they still landed without a sound on her solid wood floor. The lovers didn't stop to gather their clothes, just ran for the door.

Click-drag-clank.

They stilled, turned. In their dash, they had taken their eyes off their pursuer. Alexander flowed from *chasse* to *grand jeté,* taking a powerful flying leap, leading with a pointed metal toe at chest height. Carlotta and Henry grabbed for each other, twirling out of range of the berserk clockwork man's dangerous appendage. Alexander landed with a clang and rounded to face them in *relevé.*

"I'm afraid I simply can't stay," Henry answered her question from before the attack began. "I have other obligations."

Alexander moved his right foot in circles on the ground, as if preparing. Carlotta kept an eye on him while she addressed the natural-born man. "The Lady Anne, you mean." For the first time, she spoke the woman's name to Henry. She'd tried to ignore reality, the fact that the lords could keep women like her as mistresses but had familial duties she couldn't fulfill. But she didn't want to be a mistress. She wanted more.

Henry sighed. "Only in my father's mind. The tyrant has decreed that I wed or be banished to Ireland on my twenty-fifth birthday."

Gingerly, they stepped towards the statue-still Alexander. Had his power run down at last? Then Carlotta could discover where her manufacture had gone wrong. She could fix this.

"How much time do we have before you must go?" she asked. To Ireland, or to a wife, it didn't matter. He would be gone. She'd be damned, though, if she didn't enjoy him while she could.

He took his eyes from the metal menace and turned to her, eyebrows down-tilted. "Happy birthday to me," he whispered.

How cruel to start a liaison just when he has to leave. Yet, she remembered his melancholy the night before and realized it for what it was. He hadn't meant to lead her on, but rather to take what pleasure he could before it was too late.

Only a few feet away, the *danseur noble* jumped high, oblivious to their emotional plight. Performing the *tours en l'air*, Alexander turned like a screw drill. The room whistled with his speed.

"Marry me, then!" she offered while running to avoid the automaton's whirling death. She didn't care that they'd only known each other a few days. "Marry me instead, and we'll dance together forever!"

Alexander's spinning grew yet faster, but Henry dodged away and pushed Carlotta to the other side. Still spiraling, Alexander punctured the wood planks and penetrated deep into the ground, stopping with only his head and shoulders visible.

"Yes," Henry agreed, face split by a wide grin. "I'll marry you."

Reaching into Alexander's chest cavity, she firmly tugged the power pack loose, surprised to find it full after all that movement.

He continued, "I'll get you real dancers, a whole company, so we don't have to rely on these unpredictable machines."

If he thought human dancers predictable, he'd learn. "And where will you get these pinnacles of grace and skill?" She'd seen no evidence of his own money, and surely his father would cut them off as soon as he learned his son had refused the Lady Anne.

Henry sailed across the separating space and whisked her into his arms, words and plans tumbling from his lips. She only caught the end of his excited speech. "And if we do as he wishes by taking the post in Ireland while you tour your ballet through those troubled counties, I'm sure Father will be pleased enough with his only son." He pecked her joyfully on the cheek. "How do you feel about being a countess in a few years?"

And with that confirmation of nobility, patronage, and wealth they sealed their fates with a kiss.

ON THE CURIOUS CONDITION OF THE ANACHRONISM IN MODERN AVIATION STRUCTURES

First Mate Jess Priory breathed deep of the clean breeze that crossed the deck of the *Aer Nova*. Far above the belching coal towers and toxic stacks, an airship floated in its own perfect world, only rarely needing to land for trade or supplies. Today's landing, thankfully, didn't proceed all the way down to the ground.

She bellowed out the captain's order to the aviators on deck. "Deeeeeee-FLATE! Thirty-five pee-ess-aye in thirty!" Moments passed, but the ship did not descend. The main balloon remained at full pressure.

Captain Mansfield didn't turn to look at her. "Best go see to the men, Mister Priory."

Jess's ears burned and she dug fingernails into her palms to keep from losing her temper. An officer should be able to handle the common aviators, yes, but a helpful word from the captain wouldn't go amiss. "Yes, sir."

She strode across wooden planks towards the ropes and riggings that allowed for miniscule changes in balloon pressure. Far faster than many on board, Jess shimmied up hemp handholds to reach the main gasket. From this position she ordered, "Deeeeee-FLATE! Thirty-five pee-ess-aye in thirty! Twenty-five in forty!"

But she wasn't going to wait for the men to start. The *Aer Nova* planned to land, even if she had to do the jobs of five aviators all on her own. She turned a knob to open a small hole in the belly of the bubble, then darted down the rigging to amidships, where she could accurately test the rate of deflation. Down five psi in twenty seconds. Acceptable, but not ideal.

On the return, when she reached the main gasket again, one of the aviators stood in the position already. "I'm here to do my job, miss," he said.

She frowned, tilting her chin and lowering her eyebrows. "That's 'Mister Priory' to you, airman." No matter her sex—proudly displayed with a tightly corseted waist and a long fall of braided hair that didn't look at all like a Chin queue—her rank made her more than equal to everyone but the captain, and the men needed to respect that.

He shrugged and lazily turned the spigot. "Yes, sir, Mister Priory." The insubordinate bastard hadn't snapped to, but she'd call him good enough for now.

Back amidships, another aviator called, "Thirty psi and falling."

They're doing their jobs, but do I have to shame them into following orders every time? If she ever witnessed them giving the same hazing to the ship's second officer, a green Leftenant named Castell, she'd be tempted to leave them all in port.

Now that she'd got them started, the landing went smoothly. They touched chrome plating on the *Perpetual Platform* floating above the city, London's knock-off of the *Punters' Platform* out in colonial Boston. Local crews immediately began work on the *Aer Nova*, since Captain Mansfield was a customer in good standing who always paid his bills in full and on time.

Aviators checked in with Jess sporadically, and she had to chase some down as they tried to disembark. She made sure that she knew where each one went; that they knew the ship lifted again in four hours; and that every airman got his ration of gold and rumbullion. They filed past her, some mumbling and others boldly stating their intentions for the whorehouses, as if to shock her like some sheltered dame who'd flush at the mention of a prostitute. She'd known a number of madams in her years, a fine and upstanding lot of savvy businesswomen.

After Jess had accounted for every common aviator on her manifest, the second officer joined her on the deck. "Going into town, Leftenant?" she asked.

He shrugged. "Not interested. Looking forward to our next voyage. Madrid, you know."

They both kept an eye on the repairs and the stacked cargo till Jess's attention turned to a blond man struggling up the ramp. He was weighed down by multiple sacks and hobbling as he dragged a mahogany trunk, so she couldn't tell his exact size, though he had to be strong to carry so much luggage. More muscled than some of the new men aboard who had yet to build up the necessary sinews, but not above the old hands who could climb a mast or load cannon by feel.

He scraped to a stop in front of her, forehead glistening with sweat and manner radiating a doughty competence. "My compliments to the captain," the man wheezed, still out of breath from his trek, "and does he have space for one more? I'm prepared to pay if we lift off in five hours."

Captain Mansfield had hired a cabriolet from the *Perpetual Platform* and gone into the city to shift their legal goods, like Indian silks, and their illegal goods, like

Haitian coffee beans. Surely he wouldn't mind if she negotiated a rate for a passenger. "The captain is indisposed," she told the handsome blond. "And lifting in five hours may be difficult. How much are you willing to pay?" She felt not the slightest remorse for creating scarcity where none existed before.

They haggled their way to a price that pleased Jess, who expected that the ship would rise smoothly in four or less. "A pleasure doing business with you. I'm the first mate, Jess Priory, and this is our second officer, Leftenant Castell. Welcome to the *Aer Nova*. Follow me, and I'll show you where to stow your things." She led him past the Leftenant, who discreetly clasped her shoulder and slanted a look at the new passenger. *Really!* She didn't sleep with every appealing man who came aboard. Though, now that Castell pointed it out...

"I'm Doctor Thomas Wadham." He'd got his breath back, and Jess could hear a deep timbre heretofore obscured by gasping. Considering that he now seemed in fine cardiovascular form, even though she'd let him lug his own stuff through the ship, she had to wonder how long he'd been scraping along the *Platform*.

"Well, Doctor Wadham." She opened the door to a small room next to the captain's quarters and across from her own and the Leftenant's. By rights, it should belong to a cabin boy, but they didn't have one, and she wanted to put the aristocratic academic in officer country, where he'd be less likely to get into trouble. "This is you." She pulled one of her braids forward over her shoulder and played with it in a coquettish manner she'd once learned from a lady in savage Russia. "Can I do anything to make you more comfortable?" she husked. Damn Castell for giving her the idea.

Wadham shifted from foot to foot and clasped his hands behind his back, which showed off much broader shoulders than she'd seen when he was stooped over. "Ah—hem, that is—I..." He trailed off and brought his hands back around to hover over his trunk, then pulled them back without touching anything.

Oh yes, this one will be fun to play with. She enjoyed the warm blush that rose up his straight neck and highlighted his eyes, bright with panic. Between working with airmen and visiting houses of a certain character, she'd picked up all sorts of bad manners. Not that she felt guilty about a single one.

"You shouldn't be too starved for masculine company," she said airily, as though nothing untoward happened a moment before. "Men make up the entire ship's complement, not to mention the captain and Leftenant Castell."

"Oh, dear," he said in a soft voice. "Do you get lonely?"

She'd led him into this trap, so she bit back her annoyed growl in favor of looking down and fluttering her eyelashes as demurely as she knew how. The *ship* provided her with female fellowship. Just as for every other man on the zep. "Only sometimes," she offered quietly.

"Well." He cleared his throat and started twisting his fingers together.

Damn! She'd gone too far and lost him again. Giving up for the moment, she made a shallow bow. "Good day, Doctor." Then she headed back to the gangplank. She had aviators to corral. *This time tomorrow, we'll arrive in Madrid.*

* * *

A job well done, Jess congratulated herself four-and-a-half hours later. All the men had returned to the ship prior to the captain's arrival, so she had the chance to show off her organizational skills. Aviators could be a rowdy lot, but none wanted to be left behind.

The captain had also been pleased that she'd contracted a passenger, which sweetened the take from London. She'd helped him store the opium powders and tinctures behind false panels in the hold, and then she'd gone to take a short kip. A meal and a nap would put her back on duty after the two-hour changewatch. She didn't want Castell bringing the ship into port tomorrow.

The doctor already sat at the small table in the otherwise empty mess, hunched over a diary with a sharpened charcoal block in his hand. After she acquired her bowl of thick soup with chunks of unidentifiable meat from the cook, she headed his way. She leaned over him to get a better look at his paper, one braid sneaking over his shoulder to brush the pages of his notebook. No one kept secrets from First Mate Jess Priory, not even well-formed passengers.

And what a secret! The paper he bent over so innocently was inscribed with the partial letters of a pieced-together circle cipher. Every aviator knew how to recognize any fragment of a circle cipher and what it meant, even if it couldn't be translated from a document's single scrap. *Mutiny!*

He'd only been on board for a few hours, and already the man involved himself in mutiny somehow. She wouldn't have it. Not on her ship. She'd drag him to the rails by his pretty blond hair and throw him overboard before word got back to the captain. And to think that she'd been on her way to *liking* him!

Wadham jumped, and only sure footing enabled her to keep her bowl from spilling. "Afternoon, Doctor." She bared her teeth in a predator's smile. "I see you're working with circle ciphers?"

His hands stilled in their scramble to cover his tell-tale scraps of paper. Though, now that Jess looked closer, she saw that they weren't scraps, but a whole sheet. *Odd.* How did the disloyal rats plan to spread out their traitorous responsibility amongst all parties if one man had all the pieces? *The dogs can't even mutiny without honor.*

"I beg your pardon," he said, "but do you know what this is?" He tilted towards her with a manic energy, charcoal tapping anxiously on the table.

"Tell me where you got it," she challenged. Would he guard the mutineers, or would he prove his own blamelessness by unwittingly giving away their plot? Only an innocent would tell her the names of the involved. As for a guilty man, well, either she'd get him on conspiracy charges, or the conspirators would kill him in his sleep.

He rubbed the chalk between his fingers and wouldn't meet her eyes. *Culpable.*

He whispered, "You mustn't tell anyone else, but... I stole it in London." He traced over a quarter-letter with a finger. "Fat lot of good that it did me."

She relaxed onto the bench to his left, putting her bowl on the table now rather than holding it as a boiling-hot weapon. She should have realized he was too recently arrived to be the center of a mutiny. Plus, his guilt over such a small infraction was delicious. "So long as you didn't get it on board." She let their sides touch when she took a sip of soup. This close, she saw a bead of perspiration trailing down from his temples, telltale of his anxiety over the fresh theft. *I wonder what he'd do if I licked it off.*

"It's from my, ah, place of work. Have you seen its like before?" He pushed the page towards her, encouraging her to take a look. "I couldn't find anything on it at the Royal Society's Library."

Never in her life had she imagined someone smart looking to her. Sure, she could read and write and sum, but her further education stopped there. Aviating took brains, but not that kind of schooling. She'd only made first mate by field promotions and foreign testing—which had its own standards—knowing she couldn't sit the British exams with all the rhetoric and studious gentlemen who knew the answers by rote but could barely twist a spigot.

If he really didn't know what he had, here was a chance to impress him with her mental prowess. Possibly her only chance ever. "I can't do much without the other three pages."

He reached into a satchel by his feet and pulled out a few more sheaves. He threw back his shoulders defiantly. "I have seven more." *Oh ho! A master thief now.* "And another set in my cabin."

She nodded and took the pages, enjoying his pride in this minor espionage. She made quick folds in the papers, ignoring his fluttering hands attempting to both protect the sheets and spur her agency. The first letter fixed, she showed him the simplicity of the cipher: Each letter in the alphabet was quartered, then given to a different mutineer or put on a different page. Lining up the quadrants rendered the letters readable.

Excited, Wadham snatched the papers from her hands. "Terribly sorry," he said when he noticed his snagged pages had sliced open her finger. He pulled a kerchief from his pocket and dabbed at the welling blood. No new plasma surfaced, and he looked up to tell her, "Not a mortal wound." Nonetheless, he didn't let go her hand nor return to his hastily retrieved code. They sat, side by side, blood to skin, and Jess knew that this was the tunnel of sound pulp novelists spoke of, a space where everything was muted and her focus stayed entirely on his Tesla-spark blue eyes.

She pulled her hand back after an unknown period and returned to her noticeably cooler soup. With a choking cough, Wadham busied himself in his work again. She watched from the corner of her eye.

Feverishly, he folded and unfolded, in between jotting down notes of the letters. Some of them looked more like squiggles than alphabetics to her, but who knew the minds of scholars? Especially members of the Royal Society. She caught him looking back at her and hastily turned her attention to the liquid in her lunch bowl. Her stomach tightened, and not from the soup. He *was* interested, after all.

"It can't be," he whispered, talking more to himself and his notes than to her.

I wonder what he's found in those pages. She didn't get a chance to ask. Clanging bells rang from above, and she stood, soup mostly finished anyway. "You should go back to your cabin and work from there, Doctor," she told him.

He began to gather up his papers. "Oh, is that the end of a shift?"

Not in the slightest. "Something like that." No need to worry the passenger.

He made a small bow. "Good day, Miss Priory."

She didn't correct him, only followed him out sedately and then ran for the top deck the moment he left her sight. The deck was chaos. Leftenant Castell was a quick study, but inexperienced in the ways of aviation, and the captain was busy driving an unplotted course by use of propellers and rudder sail alone, barely avoiding the slowest of the warning cannon.

The crew scrambled all over the deck. Some held on to wooden firm-aments, others screamed obscenities at the oncoming ships. None, it appeared, could be arsed to remember their places. She drew a breath and shouted loud from her solar plexus, "BATTLE stay-SHUNS! Move. Move. MOVE!"

The men heaved to, heading to their places above and below. Castell was the only one who looked thrilled to see her.

"Leftenant," she spoke at normal volume. "My compliments, and please gather cannon and projectiles from the Armory."

He saluted, and she left him for the gunnery deck.

She walked the short rows of cannon, yelling all the way. She'd bully the layabouts into submission this once, and they'd take it because soldiers couldn't afford the sort of lax discipline they'd been giving her. "All right, you sons of bitches. As far as you're concerned, those short stacks next to you are all the cannon we have, so these broadsides have to count. You fire when I say fire. You aim where I say to aim. Are we clear?"

Their response was a sullen and echoey, "Yes, Mister Priory." She'd take it. They were stuffing the balls and the powder, and none had gone off early yet. Yes: she'd take it.

She looked through a false gun port, matching their current speed and heading to her mid-watch reckonings. She set the aim, then called, "On my mark. Three, two, one, MARK!"

With a resounding thunder, the guns jerked backwards into the aisle and wafts of grey-white smoke drifted in through the ports. The men looked out their holes, checking to see the damage to the oncoming enemy. *Lazy bunch of lick-finger shifters.* "Re-LOAD!"

A ball rolled past her, fumbled by a less-adept aviator. She picked it up and bounced it in her hand, fancying that it gave her a maniacal look.

A finger tapped her on the shoulder, and she turned to see Leftenant Castell. His mouth moved, but she couldn't hear a thing. Holding up a finger, she called to the gunners, "On my mark. Three, two, one, MARK!"

The second volley flew, and now Castell's ears rang as much as her own. Exactly what she wanted.

Castell handed her a cannon ball, then waited.

"What's this?" she yelled.

He shook his head. "All our balls," he called back. Then he looked over at the gunners. As loud as he could, he yelled, "Reload!" She'd help him learn to get more volume, but for now it was enough.

"Will we have to shoot knives?" she asked. Shooting cutlery could only be a last choice. Sure, it demoralized the enemy and often killed a few, but the damage was minimal and the winners had a lot of trouble eating.

"Well," he hedged. "We have a lot of arrows." He mimed pulling a long bow.

Arrows! The two ships in pursuit were 200 to 300 feet away, decent distance for hollow ball cannoning, completely lousy for a ship of amateur archers. *Hellfire.*

An aviator fresh from the top deck joined them. He didn't start with a *Compliments from the captain.* At first Jess took this amiss, but then she told the man to speak up and repeat his message.

"The captain's dead, sir! Broadside took out the window and the back of the steering tower, with Captain Mansfield in between. We need you upstairs, Captain."

Oh, for fuck's sake. She didn't want a ship of her own, and certainly not this ship, especially right now. The exams alone! But there was nothing for it. Someone had to be in charge.

She nodded tightly. "Leftenant, you will stay here and coordinate the cannon. Airman Barrington," she ordered the bearer of bad news, who looked surprised that she knew his name, "go apprise our passenger of the situation and ask him if he has any ideas about arrows." To Castell she explained, "The doctor is an historian."

Then she abandoned the gunnery for the danger of the top deck.

* * *

The white flag of truce went up on each of the two enemy ships. They'd made their point and now wished to parley. In Naval semaphore, they suggested that she send out Leftenant Castell and Doctor Wadham, whereupon the *Aer Nova* would be towed back to the *Perpetual Platform* and all her repairs made at no additional cost to her crew.

Jess didn't buy that for a minute. But at least now she knew this wasn't about the Haitian coffee beans. Captain Mansfield would've been so disappointed.

The airman she'd sent below reported back to her. "Your doctor is a genius, sir, but he says he needs another hour or two." With that unhelpful tidbit, he resumed his place on the deck, gossiping with all his mates as he passed. She could only hope that Barrington was saying positive things about her and that Wadham's arrow-intensive plan didn't require her personal attention. *My doctor, indeed.*

When in doubt, stall. If Wadham needed two hours to get them out of this cozy mess, then she'd give him two hours. She pulled out the semaphore flags, which thankfully hadn't blown away, and sent her message. "Willing to discuss. Send two officers from each ship."

She collected her Leftenant on the way down to the galley—no Officers' Mess on this old lady—but he didn't seem to have any idea why he'd be a wanted man. If she was any judge of character, and she was, the man's bewilderment was genuine. Well, that gave them a question to ask when their guests arrived. Between the other captains' getting put together, and her own crew's laughable slowness in mooring their pods, she figured she had some time before she had to play host.

Enough time to set out a tea service.

Eventually, the four so-called guests arrived, two from each ship. One of the visiting captains, a tall and broad man with dark hair and a bounce in his step, put a friendly arm around Jess's shoulders. "Glad to see such civilization on a ship like this," he boomed.

His ship might dwarf the *Aer Nova*, but that was their only difference as far as she was concerned. But no, she couldn't throw him off for condescending to the old lady. She had to keep him here. "Tea and sugar?" she asked, leading their party to the sideboard.

Seated and stirring, Jess had no idea what to say. Usually, Captain Mansfield led these sorties, him being well-bred and versed in the arts of polite conversation. She kicked Castell in the ankle.

"Hello again, Jack," Castell said, nodding to the other ship's captain, a man wearing a powdered wig even on this hot day and coming from a breezy top deck of high winds. Jess was going to kill him when these men repaired to their respective ships. He'd convinced her of his innocence, but here he knew one of their adversaries!

"Mother and Father respectfully request that you cease this childish rebellion and return home," said Jack.

Ah. She could rest easy that Castell's problems, unlike Wadham's, were part of a family squabble, rather than stemming from legal difficulties. Infighting, Jess could handle. "We're quite happy to have him where he is."

"I'm sure you are." Jack gestured at the long, pitted trencher, adjusting his dainty posture on the bench.

Leftenant Castell rocked the table with the force of his standing. "No call for bad manners. Captain Priory deserves respect!"

Jack pulled out a kerchief to gently daub the table beneath his tea cup, pointedly leaving it on the surface before resting an elbow on it. "Terribly sorry, *Captain.*" His tone and his eyes belied his words. "But my younger brother belongs in Her Majesty's Navy. None of this faffing about in aviation, much less on a boat not in the Aerial Corps."

Castell's fist hit the table, sloshing tea. "Ship!" he yelled.

Jack took a sip, peering off into the beams creaking over Jess's head. "Quite."

You gonna toss your pretty hair and sniff at us? Appreciating the distinction between stalling and airing family affairs, Jess pulled her acting first officer back to his seat. She chose to ignore the pointed eyes trying to burn through her hand on his arm. *Just try and make something of that. You want to fully insult a ship's captain, you poncy bastards? Bet you can't.*

"Well, well," bellowed the darker captain in cultivated affability, "no cause for squabbles, man. Let's keep the captain obliging and hope she'll hand over her passenger."

At that captain's elbow, standing behind him more like a functionary than an executive officer, a void of a man nodded. He had no distinguishing characteristics—not tall, not pale, not sharp-nosed—just a general agreeableness that floated about him. *Nod, nod, nod.*

Airman Barrington hurried in and whispered to Jess, "Whenever you're ready, ma'am. Sir, I mean."

Jess stood. "This has been lovely, gentlemen. But I think we must agree on our inability to achieve a solution. Let me escort you back to your away pods." She didn't want these bastards on her hawk any longer than she had to entertain them for the sake of providing a diversion.

"No." The shorter, wig-wearing officer who'd accompanied Castell's brother refused to move from his chair. *A three-hundred pound block of implacable ice.* "We leave with Wadham."

"And Alfred," insisted Jack.

The overly familiar captain waved his arms expansively and slurped a hearty draught to the dregs of his cup. "Come, come. No need to fuss. Let's just finish our tea and be on our way, shall we?" He arched an eyebrow at Jess as if to say, *We are reasonable men. You've nothing to fear.* But she knew that he really meant, *Just give me a moment, and I'll find a way to take what I want and leave you nothing, lower-class scum.*

The unmoving, wig-wearing executive officer refused to be dissuaded. He pulled a flintlock from his greatcoat, previously hidden beneath too-bulky cloth. "Wadham or your life," he threatened Jess, menacing her with the pistol.

No one had ever pointed a firearm at Jess Priory. Swords, daggers, rocks, cannon... but not musketry. It was faster than those others, certainly, but no more nor less deadly. "No," she said.

She saw a flinch on his face at her unexpected obstinacy, and then Leftenant Castell pushed her down. She hit the deck as Castell leapt over the table to scrabble with the brandisher, and his connections did him some good stead. The armed man's captain, Castell's brother, jerked backwards on the man's elbow to prevent the powder from igniting in her aviator's face.

Then the pair of wig wearers tripped over one another and the rickety bench they'd been drinking tea on moments before. With a *whuff* of breath, they tangled to the floor. And with a hardy *bang* the gun discharged its load, ricocheting off a bronze pan and lodging in the door.

Everyone stilled at the sound, knowing that the entire crew of the *Aer Nova* was likely on its way down to defend from these enemy boarders.

Barrington appeared in the doorway, the first of her aviators to arrive.

"Airman Barrington will escort you back to your pods," she informed the intruders from her place on the floor. "Along with an armed contubernium." Admittedly, the *Aer Nova* didn't carry anything so organized as actual contuberniales, but she believed Barrington could find eight men to loom over these unwelcome visitors.

* * *

"I'm truly sorry for your unfortunate familial shortcomings," Jess told Castell as they opened the door to the gunnery.

"Me too," said Castell. "And they wonder why I didn't join the Navy with them."

With a wry tilt to her head, Jess turned from her first mate and beheld *It*.

It stood on a cannon's wheeled base, but with the mortar itself sheared off. It was sloppily soldered with a spare navigation wheel attached to its side, and a giant recurved bow fronted it, looped on at the grip with chrome and hemp. The size of a small pony, *It* was covered in gears and boxes of who-knew-what.

Shirtless and gleaming, Wadham popped up from behind his contraption. His blond locks were flattened against his forehead, but his glasses kept him from looking quite like the aviators at his side. "A gear gun!" he said. "Isn't it glorious?"

One of the burlier aviators slapped him on the back, and they grinned at each other in some masculine bonding rite. Across the room, another of the airmen—*her* airmen now—called, "Almost finished with the second, Doc!" *Leave him alone for two hours and he's already earned the goodwill of my crew. If this affects the enemy, he'll deserve it.*

"How does it work?" she asked.

Wadham bounced on his toes even as he shrugged back into his white shirtsleeves, covering up all that glistening flesh with a hint of propriety. She'd mourn the loss later. "You turn the wheel." He demonstrated. "Then the crankshaft pulls an arrow from the bin beneath, at a rate determined by the side wheels." His barely-contained energy and astoundingly sexy brains might keep her and her crew from certain destruction. "We can pick them off at four hundred yards, ten to fifteen targets per minute."

A better rate than the cannon! Though not nearly so destructive. Unless killing their captains would lead the opposing officers to choose to surrender. "One of the visitors went by the name Jack Castsell. Do you know him?"

Wadham ran a hand across his damp head. "He works for the History Directorate at the Royal Society."

My thief started his career large. "I don't think you're a member in good standing any longer." Jess turned to Castell. "Are you able?"

Her first officer snapped her a very smart, very Naval salute. "Yes, sir!"

He'll mourn this irreparable break with his brother later, but his dedication proves that his family raised officer material. She said, "Then I leave the gunnery in your capable hands."

She exited to the sound of "Three, two, one. Mark!"

She detoured by Captain Mansfield's cabin for his spare spyglass, then made her way to the top deck. From a distance, the enemy ships looked undamaged, but their cannon fired only quarter rounds, and their rudders shifted with the wind rather than with purpose. Raising the glass, she could see the litter of bodies from the earlier canon fire on the rival decks.

A fresh volley erupted from the *Aer Nova,* not canon but arrow. At this range, her gunnery couldn't miss. The weaponry arced through the air like dancing birds, one arrow following the next in quick succession till the enemy went all ascramble to take cover. This was a revolution in aerial firefighting!

She trained her glass more closely on Captain Castell's ship. The balloon was losing psi and slowly sinking. Her Leftenant's brother had been shot twice in the knee and the shoulder, but still lived. Flesh wounds.

Her top-deck aviators all stood at the rails, squinting at the other ships and unsurprised about the arrows. *Of course they know what we're doing. Ship gossip travels faster than steam.* "Are they planning to surrender, Captain?"

Once spotted, all the men mobbed her. She barely understood the questions. *Are we leaving? Are we winning? Do the devils hope to skin us? Did the Leftenant knock up some fancy man's daughter?*

She didn't know what answers to give them; she could barely process the words they asked. But one word stood clear above the others: the address they used. These aviators called her *Captain.* They listened to her speculative words about the situation. Somehow, in the mayhem and

157

the appointment of Wadham as Acting Armory Officer, they'd deemed her worthwhile.

She saw a third ship rising from the plains of Sheffield below. It wasn't near enough to cause trouble yet, but it could be a reinforcement. These aristocrats from the Royal Society had brethren, while the *Aer Nova* flew alone.

Jess bounded to the bridge, still the highest point on the top deck. Across from her, the two ships listed dangerously. *Will they hit each other before someone takes control and navigates them to the ground?* She needed to be lighter, faster, and gone. Two enemies had been defeated; she had no desire to take on any more.

"In-FLATE!" she called to her crew. "Up ten pee-ess-aye in twenty!"

"Aye, Captain," came the snappy reply. And in twenty seconds, her ship began to rise. Lighter, faster, smaller than any pursuers.

The *Aer Nova* set course for France. If she planned to keep Wadham, as she'd now committed, the First World would have to wait. No more Spain. No more Italy.

She'd decide their next course when they set down above Provence. For now, she wanted a shower and maybe a celebratory drink of Mansfield's sugarcane whiskey.

* * *

Bottle in hand, she emerged from Mansfield's cabin into a gaggle of aviators. Pounding each other on the back and crowing of their good fortune, they surrounded Doctor Wadham, whose manic smile and sweat-flattened hair begged for rescue. *Well, either for rescue or for a higher level of carousing.*

Jess waggled the whiskey and tossed it to the airman in the lead. "With my compliments for a job well done," she said. Then she snaked a hand through the group and closed her fingers around Thomas Wadham's wrist. "But I think I'll steal your guest of honor for a while."

The men correctly interpreted the gleam in her eye, because they replied by gently shoving the man toward her. Caught off balance, he tripped into her arms, and the men made sure to pass too close and keep him where he was, his strong muscles pressed against her own lithe frame. Heat and triumph carried his scent, and she buried her nose in his hair when next he rocked forward.

After her crewmen had passed, Wadham made as though to pull away, but she kept her fingers locked hard around his wrist like an iron clamp. Squirming a bit in her grasp, too polite to actually extricate himself, he said, "Terribly sorry." Or, perhaps, he was happy with his situation and simply thought he ought to apologize? Yes, that was it. With pupils blown and breath too fast for a man who'd been standing still, his body exposed his interest; only his mind stood in the way.

"Shut up," she said, pulling him across the short corridor to her own room. He fairly radiated energy and anticipation. Oh, she'd give him a chance to say no, but she didn't think he would.

She pulled open the door, led Wadham through, then slammed it and spun them both around. With a small *thunk*, his back hit the closed portal, and she pressed herself up against him till not even the thinnest sheet of copper could worm its way between their bodies.

She was only slightly shorter than he, so standing on her toes achieved the desired angle. She brought her lips down on his, hard, demanding that he cave to her pressure, but giving him the power. He could refuse her entrance to his mouth, could push her away. She'd hold this position, still as steel, until he chose to move forward. Let no one say she'd ever forced a man.

With a groan, his lips parted and his arms snaked up around her ribs to pull her closer. Her nipples tingled at this show of desire. *I knew it!* Her tongue plunged into his mouth, taking full possession and disallowing any movement of his own. She had control here, now that his permission had been given.

She bore down on him with teeth and tongue, nipping and licking and sucking. Her fingers knew the laces of a man's garments, and she stripped him of his dirty linen shirt with alacrity, glorying in the bronzed revelation of his shoulders. She couldn't help herself. She had to taste. *Salt and sweat and arrow-wielding victory.*

When she crossed his last, woolen barrier and dared touch the secret skin beneath his trousers, his knees buckled under the onslaught. She caught him around the waist with an aviator's strong arm. So responsive! She should reward such transparency of desire.

Clearly, it was time to leave the doorway for other, more convenient, surfaces.

They abandoned his clothing in the doorway. Again she grabbed his wrist, and now she led him to stand beside her washbasin, where she used palpating fingers and a soft cloth to clean and tease, enjoying his groans and his growing hardness. She spooned behind him, letting him rest against her when his body could not hold itself, letting the heat of his back and buttocks seep into her own sensitive skin. Then she reached around to smooth a sheep's intestine over the curved tip of his member.

He whined with need, and she felt a shot of molten honey run through her from stem to stern. Smiling, she bit his neck, but then allowed him to turn in her arms and press their mouths together again. *If he can do that, he can hold himself up for a few moments.* With no frills nor teasing, she divested herself of corset, chemise, and trousers. An aviator could be called upon to dress and undress at astonishing speeds, and she used that skill to her best advantage. She wanted to feel his smooth places, his soft hairs, his manly muscles... his everything.

He squirmed closer to her newly naked frame and burrowed into her embrace, and she gasped at the scrape of his stubble across her sensitive curves. *Maximal skin contact.* The slow rubbing burn made a contrast to his sloppy, gasping kisses that fell randomly across her chest and shoulders, as if he were too far gone to aim, only knowing that he wanted to connect.

She loved it. She loved everything about his reaction to her and to her jubilant lusts.

She held herself still, willing herself not to lose control in the face of his sweet attentions. She wanted this to last a bit longer, wanted this to be good for him. When his kisses turned to the frustrated moans of a man who needs more but isn't able to gain the purchase for achieving it himself, though, she took pity on him. "Patience, my doctor. Patience." Even as she spoke the teasing words, she walked him backwards to her bed. So close.

He shook his head violently, panting. "Now. Please. Make me forget."

Forget what? With a hearty shove, she sent Thomas tumbling directly onto her mattress. She slithered atop him before he had the chance to move. Her body molded against his perfectly, her friction-tortured nipples tightening and shocking a stutter into her breathing. She filled her lungs deep, somehow not gasping. "This is a time for rejoicing, Doctor. For celebrating life. Not forgetting." She claimed his mouth again to keep him from arguing. Whether a time for escaping or reveling, it wasn't a time for sophistry.

He moaned his agreement on a hot breath, and she knew he was ready. Well-teased and hardened, his body writhed to her command. Ever since she'd seen him all oiled and friendly with her men, she'd been ready. The battle itself was all the foreplay she needed.

Throbbing from her knees to her core and undoubtedly glistening, she straddled his hips and rubbed her slit against him. He arched into her ministrations, and that just made his member tug more at her nether-hairs, enhancing her sensations. Her right hand came up to brush her own breast, pulling at a nipple, giving her the extra touch she needed. Their eyes met, and she flicked the nub again—just to hear him groan, of course.

She rocked and rubbed her hips up and down, up and down, a few more times. Her hitching gasps were obscured by his throaty pleadings as she worked to moisten the sheath covering his slender, crooked rod. He made the perfect shape, and she knew they'd both enjoy this.

"Are you ready?" she asked.

He opened sex-scrunched eyes to look at her, but his gaze held no understanding, only a wild plea for more. She felt wicked and desirable and totally in control.

She slid him inside of her, using her own fingers to ease the course of his passage. Briefly, she fell forward and caught herself on the mattress beside his head. The stretching only intensified her need to have him deeper, skin to inner skin. With each inch's progress, she paused to circle her hips, first one direction and then the other. He groaned and scrabbled his fingers in her bed sheets, but not once did he arch up or attempt to pull her down. He seemed to know his place in this scenario, to know that if he let her direct their play then she'd make the stars shatter for him.

Once he was fully docked inside of her, she cried out, piercing and loud, and she spared a short moment to worry about the jokes her crew would make later. Then the tip of his fortuitously curved cock made contact with that rougher patch of skin and sinew at the front of her body, and she stopped worrying. She began to rock in earnest then, short thrusts that moved slightly from side to side, each time hitting that bundle of nerves that made her eyelids throb and her body tingle.

Rhythm. Short, short, short, long. On the long, he made a throaty scream and threw a hand up to tangle in her braids. The other roved her flank restlessly, a mind-less movement meant only for more sensation. She began to shake from the overwhelming pleasure of his hands on her body, his prick against that special place, her control over his obvious happiness. Short, short, long. Short, short, short!

She arched back, the tugging on her scalp only adding to the sensations. She saw lights behind her eyelids, like she'd sat up too quickly. Her mouth opened soundlessly, trying only to take in cool air, but somehow increasing the feeling of being touched everywhere. The air on her tongue and palette seemed like an extension of their coupling, like more of him on her. His heat inside of her radiated through her whole body, then outward to meet with the external stimulation. Heat and touch exploded against each other.

At once, everything was too much, and her whole body strained until every muscle tensed—*arrived*—and then relaxed. Her inner walls trembled around him, and the force of her orgasm and her pulsating aftershocks pulled him along with her.

She lowered her torso onto his, gasping with every minute shift of his member inside of her. She'd slip off him in a moment, but right now, she needed to breathe.

* * *

Jess opened her eyes to her bed's jiggling. "Give me a minute," she mumbled into the ticking. Her arm extended, trying to find Wadham's body and hold it close. As far as she was concerned, he didn't get to move yet. She had more fun planned. As soon as she'd rested up.

"Shhh." He slid out from under her, got off the bed, then returned to his rightful position as pillow.

Hopefully, she hadn't been unconscious for long, not if he was just now disposing of their preventative aid. She ran her fingernails lazily in rigging knots on his chest, straying down to his balls and then back up. "What was that you were saying earlier? About helping you to forget?"

He tensed at her side, hardened muscles making less of a comfortable pillow. *Won't have any of that.* She rolled a testicle in her palm until he shivered and forgot to be anxious. No man could refuse to talk during a thorough fondling, so said the spy-courtesans of Nippon. "What are you forgetting?" she prompted.

His hips twitched slightly into her purposeful hand, but she stilled her ministrations. *Not till you answer, bucko.* "Where will I go now?" he asked her, reluctance warring with ecstasy on his face. "Ten years worming my way into the Royal Society, and for what? I can't research in the library. I can't publish without calling down the dogs of war."

She rewarded his honesty with a strong upward stroke that ended in her softly palming the head in a circling motion. "Perhaps not in England or Spain, but I'm sure the newly elected captain will let you off elsewhere. A doctor of your knowledge would be welcome at the Nipponese court or in the universities of the American colonials." He made a face of disgust, and she tugged hard while pointing out, "They're not complete barbarians, you know."

His eyes closed—*to avoid my gaze or in the throes of passion?*—and he shook his head weakly. "The things I stole..." His hips rolled helplessly upward into her hand, and she gave a few strokes before slowing to a teasingly gentle glide.

"They'll chase you down?" she guessed.

He nodded with too much force, the vein on the underside of his piston pulsing against her touch. "Proof of culpability. They've been watching other worlds for years, then... tweaking."

She had no idea what that meant, but this exercise purposed to relax him, not to teach her everything known to the Royal Society. To reward his talkative-ness, she tweaked with her grip, sliding and twisting the one hand, and sitting up a bit to involve the other in palpating the skin below. "Other worlds like Sweden, or other worlds like Venus?" Maybe the explanation would make more sense.

"Like other Earths," he said between panting breaths. "They have a machine that lets them watch and document, then use what they learn to change the flow of things here. How many wars have been avoided or politicians elected? Who benefits when they foresee a spike in the price of gold?"

Like choosing not to fly into red skies. *In the land of the colorblind, the trichromat navigates.*

He earned a gift for discussing this subject of his exile. She tightened her grip and sped her hand, rolling atop his legs to paint W-shapes at the base of his erection with her tongue.

Held in a place of titillation so long—and doubtless emotionally wrung out—he took little time to erupt. His white fluids soon coated his stomach and a small section of her coverlet. She grinned smugly at his glazed expression; he didn't even notice.

The ship felt quieter in the wake of his passion, no raucous yells from the frolicking nor clanging bells of warning from the top deck. She got up and brought him a washrag before lying down beside him once again, ready to take a much-needed rest.

She'd just settled herself in at his side, enjoying the feel of his stroking hand on her ribs, when a polite knock rapped on her door. "Captain?" a tremulous voice called from the hallway. *And how long have you been waiting at keyholes listening, Airman Barrington?* "We're close to France, sir, and the men want to hold a brief meeting."

She pulled on trousers and a shirt, lacing her waist cincher while jamming her feet into thick, leather boots.

A quick wash of her face, and she took one more look at the handsome, spent man in her bed. A pretty sight. "Stay as long as you like," she said, then opened the door to the hall, giving Barrington a brief eyeful of the doctor behind her.

"Sorry to interrupt, sir," he said. They walked in silence to the top deck, Jess piling her braids into a secure knot as though donning a veil of self-protection. *No matter what they want to do, I'll land this ship safely.*

On the top deck, airmen ambled about. A few of them actually stood at important posts, but most just milled about—killing time until she arrived, it seemed.

"Captain on DECK!" bellowed Barrington. Miraculously, her crew snapped to attention. *If they're hoping to see Mansfield, they'll be sorely disappointed.* The airman turned to her. He must've pulled the short straw. "Sir," he said, "we've voted and agreed that you should stay captain."

From the crowd, someone called, "Three cheers for the captain!" The rest chimed in. "Hip hip, hurrah! Hip hip, hurrah! Hip hip, hurrah!"

She recognized Leftenant Castell's voice in the crowd. *Damned instigator,* she thought fondly. "We can't go home with this ship," she pointed out. "We're *free traders* now. Are you sure you wouldn't rather sell the ship for gold and anonymity?"

Affronted gasps passed through the assembled crowd. Not that she didn't agree with them: sell off the *Aer Nova?* Leave behind the fine old lady who'd brought them through storms and canon fire? "NEVER!" they called as one.

Well, she had to at least try and talk some sense into these brutes.

She paced the rails, showing off her foolhardiness and sense of balance. All eyes were on the captain. *It shouldn't be me.* "Are you sure you wouldn't rather hire out to a new captain?"

Castell dismissed the idea. "A captain who's never fired a gear gun?"

The crowd roared their reply with him. "NEVER!"

Third time's the charm, you sorry lot. "Are you sure you wouldn't rather make Leftenant Castell the new captain?"

The crew laughed, and dashed her hopes of giving this position to someone—*anyone*—else. Of course not. With only a few weeks of experience, young Castell had no right to the post. Regardless of his society manners and his drive to learn absolutely everything she'd ever tried to teach him.

"NEVER!"

She beckoned Castell and Barrington to her rail. "Then I guess you've talked me into it!" The airmen cheered. *Ah, the fickle hearts of men.* "And my first act as captain is to make Leftenant Castell my First Lieutenant, and Airman Barrington Second Mate."

A discontented mumble rose from the crowd. *I'd hoped to avoid mutiny for at least a few days.* "What about the doctor?" The cry was taken up till all she could hear was "[mumble mumble] doctor!"

As if called by his title, Wadham appeared on deck and gladhanded his way through the throng to join her at the ship's edge. "Yes, Captain. What about me?" His tight smile could have been teasing, but she saw the worry beneath it.

"We can leave you at any port you like," she offered, even though she knew he'd be safest on the move. The men hissed. "But my aviators'd be much obliged if you stayed aboard. We might need an official historian and armory officer." *So long as he doesn't expect to share my tiny quarters every night. Though, maybe sometimes. Lots of times.*

"You're too kind, Captain Priory." He dipped his head in acceptance of her offer.

"Well, *Aer Nova*." She leapt down to the deck and raced to the steersman's bridge. "Let's sail into that rising sun. Doctor, how do you feel about publishing your account of the gear gun from the shores of Nippon?"

Wadham saluted her.

"You heard the captain!" Castell yelled as loud as he could. "In-FLATE! Forty pee-ess-aye in ten!"

It's good to be captain.

DOROTHEA FRANKLIN'S MARVELOUS MACHINE

Dorothea Franklin strode through the growing puddles between the cobblestones of Whitehall. Her black umbrella kept out the rain, allowing her to hold her straight posture, a contrast to the huddled and hunched Londoners whom she outpaced, heeled boots or no.

Down an alleyway very near to Number 10, she stepped up to a brick wall and rapped smartly on the surface with the hilt of her umbrella. Invisible seams parted to reveal a staircase leading down to the undoubtedly cozy rooms underneath the Lodge's public floor. Dorothea had never been to the London branch, but the directions from the Grand Master in Boston had made the trip relatively easy.

She handed her wet umbrella to the doorman at the stairwell's end, then sought out the front desk. Her low heels clacked against the polished parquet floor until she stopped in front of a hopeful Novice. "I should like to see the Grand Master, please," she said. The young man's eyes widened, and his mouth opened, though no sound came out. "I'm from the Boston Lodge. Dorothea Franklin."

The young man inhaled with a hissing sound. *Civility through the enamel on his teeth.* Then he bowed. "I'm terribly sorry, Madam Franklin, but His Worshipfulness isn't available at the moment."

She spotted some overstuffed couches near the sherry and port table. "I'll simply wait for him here. Thank you for your help." She settled herself on the leather and velvet and arranged her cotton skirts so that they'd dry out quickly.

"But, madam!" The young man followed her across the room so as not to shout and ruin the peace. "The Grand Master is in a Cabinet meeting. He may not return for hours yet."

"No matter," she replied, patting at her curled hair. "I have no other plans. Although..." The young man bounced eagerly at the thought of sending her away. "Is your kitchen still open? I haven't had a bite since dinner on the airship last night."

He schooled his face into an insincere expression of abject apology, then lifted his eyebrows and made shooing motions with his arms. Dorothea turned to look behind her and discover at whom he'd been gesturing, and saw a dark-haired man approaching.

He wore a navy three-piece suit with a tie in the Windsor knot rather than the currently fashionable ascot. He walked at a leisurely pace, holding a glass of sherry in his left hand and gesturing to his hangers on with the right. Some of his compatriots scribbled down his words in their notebooks while the others, for all she could tell, simply admired his pink cheeks.

The man and his entourage made their way in her direction, heedless of the Novice's ever-more-frantic waving. "Ah, Nigel," the man said expansively to Dorothea's apoplectic companion, "any messages for me? None from *that woman*, I hope. Her persistence in this instance is *not* a virtue."

The Novice scratched his head. "Well, no messages, per se, Your Worshipfulness, but this lady—"

"Good, good," the Grand Master, as he must be for all that he looked barely older than forty, interrupted with a chuckle. "If I get one more telegraph about a marvelous invention from *that woman*, I shall be drowning in sour Bostonian tea."

To use such an indelicate expression in reference to my homeland! Dorothea made a face as though she'd just accidentally chewed on a sprig of caraway, thinking it was mint.

Just as she did so, of course, the Grand Master noticed her presence. "Why, good afternoon, dear lady." The way he eyed her French corset and American skirt left no doubt in her mind as to whether he truly considered her a lady.

"Good afternoon, dear sir," she parroted, likewise evaluating his decidedly unfashionable tie. She'd bet he was the kind of man who still consulted a pocket watch instead of one strapped to his wrist.

"Oh, an American," he cooed. "How lovely."

She gave him a stern look down the edge of her nose, letting him know she was not fooled. "Dorothea Franklin," she said, sticking out her hand to shake, "of the Boston Lodge."

He bent over her hand to give it an air kiss, not quite hiding his raised eyebrows and wrinkled nose on the way down. "So pleased to make your acquaintance, my lady. Please, call me Sir George."

This time, she let the *lady* go without a matching remark, since most women of the European Lodges *were* ladies. Even in the colonies, working your way into the familial circle took money as well as creative impetus. "I'm afraid my letters to you have gone astray," she said, pretending she hadn't heard his unfortunate opinions when earlier expressed to Nigel. "So I've come in person to get everything straightened out."

With perfect aplomb, he tucked her hand into the warm curve of his jacketed arm and led her away from his hangers-on, leaving them to scramble for new places in Nigel's appointment book. "Oh, *that* Dorothea Franklin," he exclaimed.

He escorted her to a private room and seated her in an antique chair with a wonderful view of opposing wall's carved wood panels, depicting the battle of King Athelstan driving the Vikings out of England; Athelstan wore a lodge ring and wielded an historically inaccurate two-handed sword.

"Yes, I received your letter and proposed press release three months ago. And every successive weekly letter, not to mention your recent habit of providing a daily tele-graph. I have been touched by your thoughtfulness." He closed the little room's door, then strode the five steps to the waist-high bar on confident, powerful legs. "But surely you were having a bit of fun with me."

She clenched her hands in her skirts. "A bit of fun?"

He paused in the midst of pouring her a glass of some-thing rich that would undoubtedly go straight to her head. "You couldn't be serious." He huffed a laugh. "Inventing a time machine and wanting to share it with the world? A jest, of course." He passed her one tulip glass and sat in the chair beside hers.

She crossed her legs to keep herself from standing up and pacing. "No, sir, it was not a joke or jest. That time machine is my *life's work*. It is my Mastery project. It will make the world stand up and take notice of who I am. 'Franklin's Marvelous Machine.' I can assure you, sir, that I have indeed built a time machine, and it works just fine!" Her voice had risen towards the end, but only slightly.

The Grand Master shook his head and picked up her hand. She snatched it back. "Dear lady," he said, "I didn't mean to imply that you hadn't invented this marvel. Only a Mason could do such a thing, and one as lovely as you surely does everything she sets her mind to."

She tilted her head, refusing to be pacified by hollow praises of her appearance. The *mind* mattered. "So why have you ignored my letters? Wouldn't you like to experience this new invention? The London Masons could use the reputation boost among the sciences, I believe."

He grinned at her, making her believe a man of mischief might reside beneath his pompous exterior. "Who says it's a new invention?"

No! It can't be! I've created something completely new and wonderful, and now everyone will know my name.

He continued. "Who says someone else didn't already invent it? Or isn't about to invent it and give it to the archives before you did?"

Beaten to it by a fellow Mason, past or present? She took a deep drink from the cognac he'd pressed into her hand, struggling to breathe. Surely, she'd have heard about it. Or her Grand Master in Boston would have. At their lofty level, Masons didn't keep secrets from each other. "Someone didn't already invent it," she bit out. "I would know."

Sir George reached over to pat her hand gently. "Now, now, dear lady, that's like saying you couldn't have invented it either."

She wouldn't be dissuaded by old logic jokes. "I would certainly pick up the hundred-pound note laying in the street, whether I believed it was there or not," she growled.

"Please forgive me," he said. "But you must admit that we certainly don't want anyone *else* to know about it."

She rocketed from the chair like she'd been given too much coal. Back and forth she paced, gamely refraining from tearing out her painstakingly-curled hair... or his dark crop. "Of course I want people to know about it! I want to save lives; I want to show the power of our order." She took a breath. "I want people to call it Dorothea Franklin's Marvelous Machine and give thanks to my memory every day for a thousand years. Yes! I want people to know about it!"

The Grand Master stood as well, a dark pillar in the middle of the room, unmoving and unmoved. "Then you are a fool," he said in a clipped tone, all his playful politeness gone. "The consequences to England alone would be astronomical. The fact that we've kept your huge marvel a secret, in the past and in the future, is nothing short of a miracle."

"To England?" Breathe, she had to breathe. She shouldn't have tied her corset so tight this morning. The French style cut across her breasts and pressed a line into her skin that went straight through to her ribs. "Who cares about England? This is the bounty of our entire world!"

He caught one of her arms as she stalked past him on her next pace through the small room. Pulled into his arms and forced into stillness, she felt the warmth of his breath against her nose and the strength of his muscles through his suit. How dare he touch her so familiarly? She twisted to free herself from this carnal prison, but his next words stopped her. The conversation was more important than the flesh.

"Imagine," he spoke clearly, looking into her eyes, though she found herself looking into corners and behind him as much as directly at him. "Imagine that Franklin's Marvelous Machine became public knowledge. Now imagine that you are a politician who just did something horribly unpopular. What do you do?"

She puzzled over the question for barely a moment. "You go back and fix it," she said. "But there's nothing wrong with that. It's better for the people."

"Colonials," he teased. "Now pretend that you're a politician who's scared to do something because you think it might be unpopular. And pretend that you think it might be unpopular because your Cabinet Secretary, also Grand Master of the London Lodge, has convinced you that it will be. In the interest of science, what do you do?"

"Test my hypothesis," she answered by rote. "There's no reason not to."

"Exactly!" he exclaimed, hurting her ears with his excitement. "And when you realize that you can do anything, without remorse?"

She tried to refuse the knowledge of human nature, and felt her erratic breath making her lungs fight against her corset once again. *No! No one would use my machine for nefarious purposes.* "But no one would believe that!" She shook her head wildly and tried to break free from his grasp. She needed privacy to gather her composure.

He pulled her closer, ending her struggles, and nosing at the hot tears that started to fall. "You can't put Pandora's gifts back in their box, my dear," he whispered in her ear.

Her machine wouldn't destroy the Lodges, it would make them stronger. Wouldn't it? Shouldn't it? On the end of a desolate scream, she pressed her open mouth to those handsome lips. He had to stop talking, stop talking, *stop talking.* The pressure of lips to lips blocked out everything but sensation, and she concentrated on that, refusing to let other thoughts or worries get in her way. She focused on the surprised way he let go of her wrists, though he didn't step away.

Her newly freed hands went to work, unbuttoning his jacket and vest, and scrabbling to touch the bare skin underneath his fine, cotton shirt. He was so warm, so smooth, so uncomplicated under her fingers. She smiled into his throat, where she nipped the skin even as her nails played with his freed nipples.

He gasped, and—as if the gasp had broken his paralysis—Sir George's arms locked again around her satin-cinched waist and forced her to straighten. Their eyes met, and Dorothea knew his roused passion would be furious and ardent. No mistaken meanings here. With fervor running hot, they would each rush the other to the pinnacle of ecstasy. No compunctions. A brief deliverance from reality.

They dove into zealous kisses, mouths open and sliding, not trying to form the perfect example of a decorous kiss, but rather experimenting in maximal touch and connection. Her heart shuddered in its corseted confines, beating hard against the satin and stays. She darted a tongue out, and he joined her; the licking added a new texture, another way to entwine as much as possible, to engage every nerve ending.

Hot. She was so hot. She'd swear she barely had a sip of the cognac. She knew that Sir George could end her overheated suffering. He could meet her on the plane of the flesh as well as he'd met her on the plane of the mind. *No!* She couldn't think about her project's fresh complications now. She could only feel.

She pushed him down onto a settee she'd passed in her earlier pacing, straddling his legs most wantonly. Sir George quickly looped one arm behind her lower back for support and used the other to pull her left breast out of her high French corset. His fingers lightly brushed over the outside of her bosom, creating the most exquisite sensitivity somehow connected to the bones of her face, making her want to open wider to receive more of the sensation, though that made no sense at all.

Then Sir George revoked his kisses, but Dorothea's dismay was short lived. His lips closed over her left nipple without exploratory licking or sucking. He gnawed gently on the aureole, and she cried out in a wordless scream; her legs automatically opened wider, pushing her down against his lap harder, an action which made her squirm as the new sensations teased at her core.

She licked her lips as Sir George made teasing flicks on her nipple. She'd never felt so aroused, never felt anything this intense... and so quickly! She'd heard at university that crying led to sensitized skin, but she'd never believed it could be true. Still, here she was, practically attacking a Grand Master and needing completion soon. Soonest!

With a light scrape of teeth, his mouth came off her bosom, and she barely felt the edge of the corset digging in to her marvelously abused breasts. Through dazed eyes, she looked down at him, wondering how she'd gone from aggressor to passive recipient of tingling pleasures.

He gently flipped her over so she rested on her back on the settee, all the power Sir George's, as it had always been. She undulated in his direction, her very essence begging for his regard.

He closed her legs tightly with his wool-encased thighs and unfastened only the necessary portion of his trousers while she struggled to open her legs again, missing the pressure against her womanly foundation. He clamped his knees outside her own and flicked her swollen nipple with his finger. Arching her back, trying to simultaneously get away from that brief snap and also to reacquire connection with the sensation, she gave herself over to whatever he wanted.

"So smart," he whispered as he paused above her. "So beautiful. So completely *brilliant.*" Moving her skirts out of the way, he wormed his fingers into position against her pearl, then lined up his naked cockhead to replace those digits on the spot.

She squirmed up against him. "Yes," she panted out.

He laid himself over her, reinstating their messy kisses and moving his right hand in circles over her already reddened nipple.

Back and forth their hips moved, first gently and then with more force. Dimly, she heard a voice whining on exhales and recognized it as her own. She wanted to look at him again, but couldn't focus on anything, her occipital nerves as overloaded as the rest of her. Of its own volition, her pelvis flew up towards his body, leaving their rhythm behind and pulsating once, twice, five, ten times.

With a last wail, she settled onto the furniture, depleted. Above her, Sir George kept up his movement, and she shuddered with each press into her over-sensitized body. This almost hurt in the aftermath, but she couldn't refuse him his pleasure. She wouldn't deny this man anything. Also, she couldn't bring herself to move.

Quickly enough, Sir George too was spent, coating her thighs in warmth and seed. Languid-limbed, he laid himself along her body as though she were an old lover. Dorothea didn't mind.

She lay on the settee beneath him, listening to his harsh breaths and fixated still on that one word he'd used. "You think I'm brilliant?" Her voice came out too weak and pleading for her taste, but the words were gone now. No sense in regretting their delivery.

Sir George's cheeks flushed pink in that way only British men could make look masculine. "Brilliant," he confirmed. "Brilliant, clever, gifted—nay, genius. And in all truthfulness, I've never seen a time travel contraption before. We don't have five or six differing models downstairs in the catacombs. Yours is the first, and that alone shows just how remarkable you are." He wrapped a hand beneath her neck and pulled up slightly as he bent closer, controlling their first *gentle* kiss, merely a meeting of lips, and Dorothea warmed to the idea that he'd kissed her without the fury of their earlier coupling.

Strangely unfocused in her post-coital lassitude, she couldn't muster the level of excitement she knew she should feel. "The only time machine. Mine. I did that."

Sir George nodded. "You know," he said oh-so-casually. "We could use a scientist of your caliber here in London. While perhaps it would be unwise to make the knowledge of your Marvelous Machine public,"—she could agree on that point now that she considered its ramifications in the hands of the unscrupulous—"you could work on some of our lapsed ventures that were given up as too impossible."

"I do quite like impossible undertakings," she said, thinking about what it would mean to achieve success on an abandoned project. Not just something that the rubes of the world classified as absurd, but something her peers believed futile. Surely, that challenge would lead to fame and recognition of her capabilities, even if her time machine could not.

"As an official maker in our Lodge," he talked business even as he grasped his pocket square and wiped the mess from their bodies, "we'd make sure you were well-equipped with anything that you needed. Perhaps I can entice you with an invisibility engine, or an ever-changing doorway?" He laughed a bit at those last words, as if they could only ever be a joke.

Dorothea didn't even know what an ever-changing doorway was, but already she wanted that project. An outcome no other scientist saw as reliable? She'd show them all.

"Of course," he continued, standing up, "you could stay in rooms here until you found a house of your own. I'm sure you don't wish to intrude upon your hosts for too long."

Actually, she'd planned to collect her small valise from the airship dock and find a boarding house after her meeting with the Grand Master. She'd made no arrangements for the trip and didn't keep any acquaintances in London, at least none close enough to impose upon unannounced. Now that she'd made contact with Sir George, though, she knew she'd be staying. What waited for her back in Boston? An invention she couldn't discuss and a laboratory she could donate to her mentor's next protégé. The position he offered in the Lodge couldn't be denied. She'd have to resign herself to being known as *the American.*

She smoothed her rust-colored, cotton skirt down to her ankles and rearranged her décolletage. "That would be lovely, thank you," she accepted, holding out a hand to shake on the agreement.

Sir George bent over her hand instead, kissing the back and then turning it over to kiss the palm. She shivered when he looked up through his sweat-curling hair to meet her eyes. "Or you could stay with me."

She retracted her hand and stood. "I don't believe that would be wise," she said. It would do her no good to give into his whims from the start. If she were to stay in London, she'd need to be respected. The other Masons would have to believe in her competence, not in her bedroom charms. "You must know that this can never happen again." She considered his well-covered chest, which she'd never have the chance to see unclothed. *Perhaps we can revisit this edict in future, should an acceptable occasion arise.*

Sir George tugged on his cuffs as though straightening them required all his focus. "Of course, dear lady."

She couldn't have him calling her by that appalling sobriquet. "Madam Franklin, please."

He gave her a small bow and a sad smile but still would not meet her eyes. Had he never been denied before? Well, he'd just have to get used to it. A handsome, powerful man had to learn some time that women wouldn't just fall into line. Some women had their own priorities.

He patted down his vest and jacket one and swept to the door, his mouth in a flat line. Sir George threw the door open and gestured her on. "Madam Franklin."

She held her giddy hopes for the future close to her heart. For the benefit of any eavesdroppers, she said, "I am quite convinced, Sir George. Shall I have the Grand

Superintendent of Works set up a temporary work-space?"

Yes, she could speak obliquely for now. Maybe in the future, she could act on the affection she felt for him. But not until she had established her place amongst the Londoners. Not until she'd ascended and all the right people recognized her as Dorothea Franklin, Grand Maker of London.

OTHER WORKS

Short stories available:
"Heir Apparent" in *Masked Pleasures (2012)*
"Day Trip" in *Sex in London (2013)*
"The Three Temptations of Mara Samun" in TBA (2013)
"Terran Export" – award-winning flash fiction, free from Circlet.com

About the Author

Photo copyright Jeremy Barton, 2012

Victoria Pond is a professional writer on projects ranging from video games to novels. She lives in Seattle with a husband and a cat, where she sings with a Celtic band and is working on the next novella in her steampunk erotica universe.